P9-CAX-661

ECCENTRIC
LADY

ECCENTRIC LADY

— Jane Lovelace —

WALKER AND COMPANY
NEW YORK

c. 1

First published in the United States of America
in 1983 by the Walker Publishing Company, Inc.

Published simultaneously in Canada by John Wiley
& Sons Canada, Limited, Rexdale, Ontario.

ISBN: 0-8027-0727-0

Library of Congress Catalog Card Number: 82-51188

Printed in the United States of America

10 9 8 7 6 5 4 3 2 1

BL

JUL 6 '83

Wealthy daughter of deceased earl, who
would rather stay at home and farm, is
packed off to London for the season.

=1=

LADY ELIZABETH ANNE Haughton-Marshall looked up as the
butler made his announcement. That the worthy servant
delivered himself of his message in a way more befitting a
London drawing room than a hen house was due to his
superb training. Why he would so demean himself as to leave
his sacred domain and journey into the stockyard on the way
to convey his message was, as he told his underlings, because
he knew his Duty, even if his employer so forgot herself as to
behave like a Hireling.

Lady Beth, as she was called by the servants and stockmen,
frowned her displeasure over the news and turned back to her
task. She was at that moment standing before a waist-high
shelf on which no less than a dozen nests were evenly spaced.
Eight of the straw-filled boxes contained setting hens, which
eyed the somberly dressed servant with such ferocity that he
backed to the door once his message was delivered. They paid
not the slightest attention to the young woman who continued with the delicate job of turning the eggs under the
hen at the far end of the building.

"Very well, Hughes, tell my uncle I will be in shortly."

Lady Beth was a woman who kept her word. To a person of
such direct nature, "shortly" meant that once the eggs were
turned to her satisfaction she would immediately repair to
the drawing room. She did pause in the boot hall to change
her soiled brogues for slippers. To have removed the stained

1

overskirt she wore in the barnyard never entered her mind. Her titian hair was twisted back and held by combs in an unfashionable knot, and several strands had escaped. Her sole effort at rearranging it was to push the wayward pieces back behind her ears.

Not even her lack of attention to her appearance could hide the fact that she was a lovely young woman. The briskness of her attitude, the swinging stride that took her without delay from one task to another, would have been both unfeminine and unattractive in most females. But Beth, a small girl with large brown eyes in an elfin face, could have been the pattern for faerie lore, and her quick, forthright action and speech only added to the gamine impression.

She entered the drawing room and marched over to the portly gentleman with no shortening of stride. "Good to see you, Uncle." She held out her hand for him to shake. "I'm sorry I wasn't here to greet you, but I was in the hen house. This new strain I'm working with is proving out nicely. Excellent layers, big broods. A little early, the weather is still a little chilly, so we have to keep them inside, but I'll have a gift for you before long. The finest group of pullets you've yet to set eyes upon."

This enthusiastic report appeared to be quite lost upon the Earl of Farling, who stood holding her hand. If he knew what a pullet was, he gave no sign of it, nor did he look as if he would care to be enlightened. As with many second sons of independent means, he had spent his time in London, neither knowing nor caring about the running of estates. The epidemic of influenza that carried away his father had taken his older brother, Beth's father, within the same week, leaving him not only with the title, but with the responsibility of trustee to his young niece. The deaths were four years in the past.

His inherited properties were looked after by his man of

business and his bailiffs, demanding no effort on his part, and he had left Beth the management of her own farms, since she had insisted on personally overseeing the labourers. Their only difference of opinion had occasioned three arguments between uncle and niece. Each spring he made the journey to Carthalin Hall in an attempt to persuade Beth to spend the season in London.

Beth had no doubt but that this visit was prompted by his desire to see her make a formal entry into society, especially after the heartrending sigh he gave as he turned over her work-roughened hand, giving it a thorough inspection.

It wasn't to be thought wonderful that a man of his address would be disturbed by seeing his niece behaving in such an unfashionable manner. True, he wasn't dressed in the affected style of a Bond Street Beau, indeed, he was too knowledgeable and too aware of his reputation as a man of the most impeccable fashion to show himself in the country in anything but the simplest of costumes, but his coat was unmistakably London tailored and his topboots had never been besmirched by the mud of his holdings. His carefully-styled white hair and his pink, smooth skin were clearly not used to harsh exposure.

"Such a poor little hand," he murmured and led Beth to a confidante, where he seated them both. "Chicken-skin gloves, my dear. Must have a pair. Just the thing for those poor little hands."

"Much good they would do me with the stock," Beth laughed. "The hens would likely take offence and stop laying."

"You've no business out with the hens," he complained. "Bad choice in workers—" He nodded his head emphatically, as if he had solved a weighty problem. "That's the trouble. Must get you some new people. Then you won't have to do the work."

"You can't be serious!" Beth looked at him with considerable astonishment. "My stockmen are the best in the county! Those my father didn't hire, I did, and either I am an excellent judge or I have been very fortunate—more probably the latter."

Lord Farling sat perfectly still, neither answering nor acknowledging her praise of her workers. He continued to keep his lips puckered, his eyes fixed on some undefined point on the ceiling. Watching him out of the corner of her eye, Beth wondered what was amiss to put him in such an unusual mood. She tried again to make her feelings clear about her employees.

"Uncle, my men do everything they are asked to do, and many of them have been here so long they anticipate me. But my new strain of hens is my special project, and I prefer to work with them myself. Why, before next summer, I am persuaded we will have the most productive broody houses between here and London."

"Yes, yes, excellent layers, excellent milkers, the best hunters, but this is no occupation for you, m'dear."

Beth arched her brows. "Do you suggest I leave the three most productive farms in Dorset and go into trade?"

He gave her a reproachful look. "There is no need for you to spend so much time on them."

Beth carefully folded her hands in her lap. She raised her chin and straightened her back. "My *father* spent twenty years making these three farms what they are, and I intend to see they remain as well cared for as when he was alive. He was proud of them, and he taught me that same pride. I can't think where my time could be better spent."

Lord Farling looked slightly alarmed. "My dear, I was not casting aspersions on my brother Charles! A good sort, Charles, always thought a lot of him. Know he brought you up to like the places, can't fault him for that. Know he taught you how to run them. Left you alone to manage them, haven't I? Not one for sticking my oar where it isn't wanted."

Like Beth he stiffened his posture. "Still, I've got a responsibility to Charles. Time I accepted it. Don't know how I've let it go so long—even Sarah will agree with me—" He looked around as if just realising his sister was not in the room. "Where is that pigeon-brained sister of mine?"

"I'm not sure I've met *her*." Beth frowned at him. "If you're speaking of Aunt Sarah, she's in Exeter shopping for muslin. I'd think you would approve. She's ordered patterns from London and plans to dress us both in the most current styles."

"About time she did something. Should have been making sure you had decent clothes before now."

At such an unjust comment, Beth's eyes flashed. "I will have you know, Uncle, that I have, and have always had a wardrobe sufficient for my needs. Do you expect me to go traipsing through the barnyard in silks and satins? If I did it would take both your fortune and mine to keep me in clothes."

"But you don't belong in the barnyard!" he complained.

"Well, that's where I intend to be," Beth retorted.

"Well, you won't." His tone became belligerent. "You have put me off for four years, girl. The first year I had to give you, of course. Not the thing at all to have a come-out in black gloves. But three more years you ignored me. Now you're going to do as you ought."

Beth turned startled eyes on her uncle. He was normally a good-natured man. Occasionally he became a little pompous when he rounded on his sister Sarah for not being more outgoing, but Beth had never seen him in a stubborn or belligerent mood, and the set of his chin at that moment indicated both. She was not one to be cowed, however.

"Though you haven't mentioned it, I take it you mean to

drag me to London for the season. What would you do, Uncle, pull me kicking and screaming into Almack's? That would be a nice picture for your London friends, would it not?" She hoped her unwillingness would give him a picture of a contretemps so odious that he would shy away from such a discomfort, but his chin only went out further.

"Time you went to London," he replied. "M'brother would have seen to it. My responsibility to get you there. Can't shirk my responsibility. If he were alive he'd never forgive me."

"Now that doesn't signify," Beth said. "If he were alive you'd have nothing to do with it." She reached over and put an affectionate hand on his arm. "Uncle, I don't want to distress you, but I really can't go this year. I'm just too busy here. As to it being your duty, why, that's silly. I'm of age and can do as I want. You haven't been my guardian for two years now."

"Know that. Not your guardian, but still your trustee." He turned his head to look out the window. "I still have control of your farms. It's a bad thing you're making me do, m'dear. Never wanted to interfere. Never wanted to have to look after the plaguey things, but it seems the only way to get you to do what you should."

Beth looked at Lord Farling, his perfect attire and his delicate-looking skin. She couldn't resist a laugh. "You're not going to manage them?"

He jumped as if he'd been shot. "Lord no! Not in my line at all. Got someone else—someone for each one."

Beth leapt to her feet, staring at him unbelievingly. "You can't do that!"

Lord Farling's eyes met hers briefly and shifted away. "Past tense, m'dear. Have done it. The two for Addiston Farms and Duchin Mills are even now on the way. Henderson, the man taking over here, will arrive by the end of the week. Don't try giving them orders. Made it plain they work for me on property in trust. You go to London, do as you should, and you can rule the roost between seasons, or until you get married.''

''And if I do not?'' Beth walked to the window and stared out at the well-tended fields. Like her father, she seldom thought of anything except them. They had been her world.

''If not, then they stay under my control,'' he said heavily. ''Don't want to do it—lot of work I'd just as soon not do, but no other way I can see to make you do as you should.''

Beth could well believe he might not relish the chore. He cared little enough for overseeing his own property, and it was she who was the terror of the Farling Manor bailiff. What would happen to her farms while she was away she dared not think. He would have done his best in choosing the bailiffs, she knew, but with his limited experience she doubted his judgement. A sly look in his direction convinced her he was past the point where she could change his mind. At that moment it seemed to her as if she must acquiesce in order to have her property back in a few months.

To the extreme left of her view she saw Greaves, the head groom, walking Lady Anne. The superb lines of the blooded hunter were at present somewhat blurred by the mare's nearness to foaling. Beth had been anxiously awaiting the time. The colt's sire was Tall Walker, a champion out of the famous Crompton Farms stables and the result of two years of dickering correspondence between Beth and the bailiff of the best stable in the country. To lose the right to see the colt born brought tears to her eyes but she shook them away.

She knew herself to be trapped, and with the sudden instincts of an animal at bay, she immediately began casting around for a means of escape. It occurred to her, however, that she must ascertain the limits of her restrictions.

''What are your terms, Uncle?'' she asked in a quiet voice.

''That you go to London, take full part in the season—that you pull no tricks, Beth!'' This last was said with some asperity as she turned to look at him. "I see the fighting light in your eye, and mind you, girl, I mean what I say! You will first give me your word that you will treat each and every eligible gentleman you meet with civility and the natural charm I know you have."

He stopped, waiting for her answer, and so set was his expression that there was nothing for Beth to do but capitulate.

"My word," she replied with grudging obedience.

"You will attend as many social activities as health and good sense allow. I've no wish to see you run into a decline, but you'll make yourself available for routs and balls."

"My word," she repeated.

"Oh!" Warming to his subject, he shifted and pointed his finger at her. "You will make yourself agreeable to the hostesses, so that you get invited."

"I will," Lady Beth answered meekly. She was beginning to wonder how many restrictions he would put on her, and if there was any way she would ever get her properties back.

"And—and clothes! You will dress yourself properly in all the latest fashions. None of these terrible things you wear in the stables, mind. You're not to take them with you. Can't think what that fool Sarah is about to allow you to run around like that."

At the second attack on her aunt, which she considered entirely unwarranted, Beth lost her meek attitude.

"Uncle, what do you expect Aunt Sarah to do? Dress me? I'm not still in leading strings, you know. You do her an injustice. She would be the first to want to see me fashionable. And she'll be after me every minute we're in London, I assure you."

"Well, she won't, because she ain't going." Lord Farling's chin was thrust out again. "Never liked London, and she never took. Even if she is m'sister, nothing but an antidote. Season after season m'father sent her. Didn't do a bit of good. Make a dashed poor chaperone to boot. Got somebody else in mind for that. Widow I know. Mousy little thing, Jane Westcott, but she'll see you get all the proper invitations, and help you know what's right. She'll help you with your clothes, and I mean it, girl, you'll not get the management of the farms after July if you don't do your part."

"I will outfit myself with taste, unless you would rather oversee my wardrobe yourself." Beth dropped into a chair and put her hands up over her face in an attempt to concentrate. In her frustration she gave out a ragged sigh that shook her shoulders and was surprised at the sounds of distress that came from her uncle. Suddenly he was at her side, clumsily patting her on the shoulder, his voice full of anxiety.

"Don't weep, child. Oh, dear, do pull yourself together, Beth."

Never in her life had Beth been missish, but discovering the effect on her uncle, she determined at once to see if anything could be gained by an affectation. Since neither she nor her aunt were vapourous women, she had no clear idea of how to go about it, but since her uncle was a bachelor and never known to be a libertine, she rather thought he would be no more expert than she.

"I declare I will never please you," she answered in a trembling voice. "It may be that no matter what I do, no one will offer for me. Some will think that to be already twenty-two and still unclaimed, I must be lacking in the qualities for a wife. I will be considered on the shelf. How will I go on? What other restrictions will you be setting on me as time goes by?"

He stopped petting her shoulder and started awkwardly tapping her on the top of her head. She almost asked him to stop, because he was causing one of her combs to dig into her very tender scalp, but only just in time she remembered her anguish should be such that she would not heed it. She felt some guilt as she heard the very real discomfort in his voice.

"Child, I beg of you, do not take on so. I'm only asking you to go to London, after all. It's not like you're leaving the country, you know. It's not India."

"How many more restrictions?" she wailed.

"None, my dear, none—I give you my word! You'll be back in a matter of months. The time will go very quickly, I assure you."

"I'll miss seeing Lady Anne's foal!" She was not at all prepared for the very real sob and the accompanying tears.

"Oh, but isn't that due any time? I certainly think you could wait until she does. Oh, child, *do* take heart."

Two gentlemen of fashion were paused at the corner of a London intersection, just trading a few parting words, when the travel-stained coach came bowling down Tyburn Road. As the dandies looked up, they lost their fashionably bored air and raised their quizzing glasses.

"I *do* say!" ejaculated the first. "Sixteen-mile-an-hour cattle, or I've never seen any!"

"All blood and bone," his friend agreed. "Look at the stock behind it! Four-in-Hand Club cattle—has to be!"

They stood and watched as the magnificent team pulled the heavy traveling coach at a pace a bit too smart for London. Behind it rode several grooms leading another team of equal quality, a pair of snow-white high steppers, and several riding animals whose lines could only be appreciated by the truly discerning.

Both gentlemen would have been surprised had they been able to see into the coach. The owner of the splendid cattle would never wear a sixteen-caped driving coat or tool a barouche at a strict trot to Salt Hill with the famous Four-in-Hand Club, but it was the circumstance of being born a female that would deny her. No member of that envied set could boast of finer stock than the young lady who sat with her feet primly close together, her hands folded in her lap. She kept her eyes on the forward wall of the vehicle, unconscious of the parlourmaid who was acting as her abigail on the journey. She evidenced not the slightest interest in her first chance to view the streets of London. At the moment she was far too occupied in her plans for making that worthy city uninterested in her.

She was a fortnight later in her arrival than had been originally planned, a circumstance due entirely to Lady Anne's delay in foaling. For that service to her owner, the mare had been rewarded with uncounted carrots, apples, and lumps of sugar until she was outrageously spoiled. Lady Beth's gratitude knew no bounds when, close on the heels of the first colt, a second and identical foal had appeared. She had stayed long enough to see them on their way to sturdy growth, a delay her uncle could not resent. As much as he desired to get his niece to London, he, too, was enamoured of the foals.

What had bothered Lord Farling was the number of horses his niece was bringing to London. At first he determined to take her to task, but changed his mind. Since he, too, had a great fondness for his favourite beasts, he decided she more than likely thought of them as pets rather than work animals and would be distressed to leave them. He knew each one to be the result of her breeding stables, raised and trained under her watchful eye if not her own hand, and he was concerned that to make her leave them behind would injure her mood in London. Had he known her plans, he would have sincerely regretted giving his word that he would put no further restrictions upon Beth.

As the coach drew to a halt outside an impressive dwelling in Berkeley Square, Beth looked out with some curiosity.

It would have been wonderful if she had not, since for more than three years the house had belonged to her, and here she would sojourn as long as she was in London. Unlike its neighbours, it had a pair of stairs ascending from the right and left, paralleling the street to a wide landing from which another flight led to the main entrance on the first floor. Beneath the wide landing, a pair of doors, separated by a wall that jutted out even with the steps, looked to be for tradesmen and servants.

After Beth's first look, she lacked the opportunity to see much else. Before the steps of the carriage were lowered, all three doors were thrown open, and each disgorged a goodly number of her servants, led by Myra, her maid. All those that appeared were country bred, brought up in service at Carthalin Hall, and their obvious joy at her arrival completely overreached the rigourous training given them by Hughes, the butler.

"My lady, we've been so worried!" Myra cried as she took Beth's arm, virtually pulling her toward the steps.

"We've been fair out of our minds, thinking you was in a ditch somewhere." Agnes, the parlourmaid, added her bit of information, shaking her dustcloth for emphasis.

Halfway up the stair, Beth paused, looking down on the assembled group that stood on the walk. Several stable hands as well as the cook and two footmen were smiling up at her. She might not be fully cognizant of all society's rules, but to be addressing servants on the street was not quite proper; still, their affection wasn't something she could ignore.

"A plague on all your foolishness," she called down. "You knew I wouldn't be leaving Carthalin Hall before Lady Anne foaled, and it was worth the staying. Mrs. Gibbs, you'd love them—two!"

The cook, singled out by name, beamed and clucked over the news of the colts. The others, heartened that coming to

London was not going to change the free and easy relationship between themselves and their mistress, trooped up the steps behind her. They crowded in, chattering about their own trip and the sights of the city.

As Beth reached the entrance hall, Hughes, who had obviously been in another part of the house, came rushing up. The sight of his staff milling around their employer more in the manner of gamboling puppies than well-trained servants, caused him to roll his eyes heavenward. His puffed up appearance gave Beth cause to believe there would be Words spoken in the Room before the day was over.

At his stiff bow she laughed and further injured his dignity by giving him a pat on the arm. "Never mind, Hughes," she said kindly. "We might still be a credit to you."

While the butler ushered the staff off to their respective tasks, Myra led Beth up to a spacious room on the second floor. Once inside, the maid stood with a certain prim stiffness that warned Beth she was expected to show her approval if she wished to remain on pleasant terms with her staff. The wallpaper had such a pale yellow background that it appeared white. On it a white latticework held small primroses, which were admirably matched in colour by the velvet hanging at the windows and on the bed. Several years before, Beth had seen this room, which her mother had used on her rare trips to town, but added to the charming decor were numerous articles that had been brought from Carthalin Hall. From the first Beth recognised the herbal scent reminiscent of her home, and noticed the lacquered box of potpourri on the small table in the corner. Several of her favourite sketches, drawn by a talented youth on the home farm, were framed and hung about the walls, and in the window embrasure her favourite writing desk had been placed to take advantage of the light.

"It could almost be Carthalin Hall," she said, watching

the stiffness in Myra relax. Her conscience gave her no qualms for the small untruth and she knew nothing could have made the maid more certain of her approval.

Beth stripped off her tan kid gloves and turned to the dressing table to remove her hat.

"Well, Myra, how am I going to like this distant cousin— my watchdog, or whatever more civil name we must call her?"

"I think it is better than that we'll be saying of her, my lady," Myra spoke up archly.

"Oh no! Not a watchdog!" Through the partially open door that led from the hallway a voice replied in strenuous tones of objection. Beth turned to see a short, plump lady, hastily pushing dark brown curls up under a fetching lace cap. The round pretty face was dominated by a pair of dark eyes that sparkled with indignation. She had pushed the door open and stood framed in the doorway, her head slightly sideways as she struggled to get one obstinate curl under the cap.

"I have quite decided that I will be a *dragon!*" announced the little woman in positive accents. "It's quite lowering, you know, to realise you're no longer a belle, and have reached the age when you wear caps and become a chaperone. I confess, when your uncle first approached me I was more dismayed than you, but I have thought of how it was when I was making my first come-out. You've no idea how odious some gentlemen can be with their haughty looks and their quizzing glasses. It's only when you can be a chaperone that you get your own back again. It will give me such a feeling of *power* to glare away ineligible suitors—" She gave a frown that was more comical than threatening. "I declare I am almost anxious for some horrid creature to come near you so I can send him on his way—"

As she spoke of coming to Beth's defence, she suited action to words and took several steps into the room. Not until she finished speaking did she realise what she had done. With a quick look around, she retreated hastily into the doorway again and looked much like a child that had overstepped the rules.

"May I come in? It's so awkward to knock on doors when they are ajar, you know."

Mrs. Jane Westcott, for it could hardly be any other, stood waiting while Beth overcame her surprise at her first encounter with her companion and chaperone. The young lady smiled, both at herself for dreading their first meeting, and at the little woman in the doorway who more nearly resembled a small, lively hen than a dragon. Beth was convinced her fire-breathing would have the appearance of ruffled feathers. She went forward with her hands held out in greeting.

From Lord Farling's description she had expected a dowdy, dispirited little woman, but the dark green muslin trimmed with a ruching of darker green ribbon was both pretty and in the first style of the day. Still, it was the expression of Jane Westcott's eyes that drew Beth's attention again. There were glints to them that hinted at far more spirit in the widow than Lord Farling had led Beth to believe.

It had never been Beth's way to dislike anyone, but being so unwillingly thrust into London, and having to accept the chaperonage of a strange woman, she had been wont to think of Mrs. Westcott in terms far from flattering and was prepared to dislike her intensely. It was an agreeable surprise, therefore, to spend the afternoon in cozy conversation. By the time the teacart had been rolled in, Beth was certain she was being instructed in the ways of the polite world, but so humourously did Mrs. Westcott point out the idiosyncrasies peculiar to the *ton,* that Beth found herself too busy laughing to resent it.

When Jane described the almost mandatory afternoon airings in Hyde Park, Beth smiled wickedly.

15

"It sounds to be just what I would most like, but though I'm country bred, I have no great love of walking. I think I must have a vehicle."

At once Jane stirred in her chair, all attention. "I knew we would deal famously. I, too, care nothing for strolling about, and like driving above anything, though I do not handle the reins myself. My late husband was possessed of little more than a competence, but he was prodigiously clever at horse trading, so we were usually turned out in spanking style when he held the ribbons. I will so enjoy riding with you."

This bit of delight brought Beth up short. On her way to London she had decided upon the type of conveyance she would purchase, and however pleased Jane might sound at the prospect of Beth's vehicle, she felt the little widow would speedily change her mind when she saw it.

Another way in which Mrs. Westcott proved herself amenable to her companion was to insist gently, though her eyes were sparkling with mischief, that after a journey of such a distance, a lady of breeding could be expected to be in dire need of rest. It would hardly be expected that she should immediately be catapulted into the rigours of shopping for her entrance into society.

Beth was more than grateful for her consideration, but the pleasant idyll lasted less than twenty-four hours, at which time Beth's youthful energy overrode her desire to put a spoke in her uncle's plans. Long used to being about the task of overseeing the work on the home farm, she found that once she had toured the house and had stepped around to the stables, she was thereafter heartily bored.

By sheer force of will she kept at home her first two full days in London. Feeling very keenly the absence of all her usual occupations, she roamed the house, getting in the way of the maids. Agnes, entrapped between her new importance at standing in for Mrs. Lovell, the housekeeper, who had stayed on at Carthalin Hall, and her fear that she might fail in her new responsibilities, rounded on Beth for upsetting the new "town" maids who weren't used to the ladies of the house poking into their duties. Even Mrs. Griggs, who usually welcomed Beth into the kitchen, was noticeably relieved when she left after a new scullery maid became so nervous she dropped a bowl and went into hysterics.

She attempted to confine herself to the drawing room where she perused a book on foreign travel. Meals were quiet, and afterwards Jane often retired to her room. Late in the evenings, when there was no chance of upsetting the servants, Beth prowled the house, peering from behind the drapes, watching the residents of the different dwellings on the square as they entered carriages or sedan chairs on their way to various evening entertainments. She envied them— not their activities, but their seeming lack of boredom.

She wondered at some length about Jane Westcott. The little woman was proving to be an enigma. Her chattiness upon their first meeting had given Beth the impression that she was a feather-headed gabster, but save her very humourous comments on the *ton* that partially veiled the underlying instruction, she had been content to sit with her interminable embroidery. Her responses when sought were charming and freely given, but she did nothing to relieve Beth's boredom. Beth had known many women of reduced circumstances who were forced to companion wealthy females, and for the most part they seemed to be convinced that a stream of nonstop chatter for the edification and entertainment of their employers was a primary requirement. It was growing obvious that Jane was not of their opinion.

Late in the second afternoon, Beth forced herself to read, in the travel book, an article on Arabia. Finished, she looked up to catch Jane's eye on her, the glint of speculation unmistakable. As Jane quickly dropped her eyes Beth felt the shock of realisation. Jane was deliberately fostering her boredom!

17

Well, we'll see who holds out the longest, Beth thought, and returned to her book. With a determination born of a challenge, she kept her lips folded primly until she retired to her room for the night. But in bed, she could not keep down the good sense that saw the humour in being aided to do exactly what she had thought she wanted, especially since she was finding it a disagreeable task.

The next morning, when the widow reluctantly announced she must attend a fitting for a ball gown, she did it with such a downcast expression that Beth found herself agreeing to accompany her chaperone to help relieve the tedium of shopping. Too late she remembered she had suspected Jane of manipulating her.

"Though why I should go to help you lighten a chore I find odious, I cannot imagine," she grumbled.

"Oh, I can sympathise with you, I truly can," Jane said as they stepped out into the morning. She threw up her hands to keep her bonnet in place as they were buffeted by a stiff breeze. "Perhaps it would be better if we were to do as much of our shopping together as possible. I do so like having someone to talk to when I am about a chore I dislike."

Throughout this speech, Jane's face had been turned to her companion, its expression one of the utmost innocence, rendered ineffective by the twinkle in her eyes.

Beth, stepping into the carriage, stopped and looked down at her chaperone with a frown. "Jane, you are the greatest humbug! I am convinced that it is only delicacy of principle that keeps you from being renowned as a gull-catcher. The world should be deeply grateful that such an awesome ability is not turned to crime."

Far from being insulted, Jane appeared thoughtful for a moment and then smiled with delight. "Do you really think so, dear? I own, at times I do wonder that people are so taken in by the least little thing." She settled herself in the carriage and nodded complacently. "It will be so comfortable, our dealing together. It pleases me to think we understand each other so well.''

A short drive brought them to Bond Street, where they dismissed the carriage after specifying a time and place for the driver to return for them. The bright, sunny day had been preceded by almost a week of damp, overcast weather, and it seemed that all of the polite society was shopping in Bond Street.

It was at once apparent that Jane had a large acquaintance among the *ton* and she was kept busy nodding, waving and greeting old friends. From their remarks Beth gathered that Jane too, had been spending some time in the country, a circumstance she had not suspected. Beth was introduced to a number of people, all of whom seemed to be on the best terms with Lord Farling and asked when they would see him in town again.

In a fashionable modiste's shop, Beth was startled as one lady, in the process of trying on a voluminous creation of silk and ruching that threatened not to contain her bulk, swept out of the fitting room and almost glared at her companion.

"Jane! Where have you been?'' she demanded in stentorian accents. "I'll expect to see you at my rout tonight.'' She swept back to her fitter again, neither giving Jane a chance to introduce Beth, nor to accept the invitation.

While Jane was fitted, Beth chose two morning dresses, a ball gown, a riding habit and a walking costume. She unequivocally refused fittings, instructing the modiste to put the garments aside. A person of great sensibility for the comfort of her servants, she had been known to forgo desired trips in inclement weather to spare her horses and coachman discomfort, and often did small menial tasks herself, rather than add to the duties of her staff, but she had no compunction at all about sending Myra to stand in for the hated fittings. Moreover, she often threatened the maid that if she put on an extra pound, she might find herself replaced. It was doubtful that Beth would have carried out the threat, but since neither she nor Myra were prone to additional pounds, the circumstance did not arise.

In the next shop, both Beth and Jane chose several evening costumes, and after sundry purchases including hats, shoes, reticules and shawls, they were just entering the carriage when the stout woman hailed them again.

"See you this evening," she called.

Jane sighed and looked over at Beth. "I think we're going to a rout," she announced dejectedly.

=2=

LATER THAT AFTERNOON, when they were having tea, a footman entered with an invitation for the rout and Beth
discovered it contained her name as well as Jane's. It was
signed by Lady Oglesby, a name that seemed to fit the overpowering woman. Beth had not been favourably impressed,
since she seldom cared for people who gave peremptory orders. Although from Jane's comment as they entered the
carriage on Bond Street she expected her chaperone would attend the rout, she herself had fully expected to spend the
evening with a book she had purchased at Hatchard's.

"I really do *not* wish to go," she said as she handed the
invitation to Jane.

"Oh, dearest, I know just what you mean," Jane gave a
sniff and tossed the invitation on the table. "She's a terrible
bore, and so autocratic, too, but I'm afraid I must. You see,
we were at school together, and she is a great friend of
Gubby's—Lord Farling. I don't dare snub her."

Beth looked up from her teacup. "You're really saying I
shouldn't either, not if I want my farms back in July."

With an exaggeration of care, as if only a considered movement of objects could direct her comments into a discreet
pattern, Jane placed her cup and saucer on the French
marquetry table and folded her hands in her lap. Her eyes, as
she raised them to meet Beth's, were cautious, with more
than a hint of apprehension.

21

"You must do as you think best, but Lord Farling will most certainly call on Lady Oglesby when he comes to town. She was originally a Ridgeley, you know.''

Jane's last statement left Beth in no doubt as to the relationship of the dictatorial hostess, or of the importance of attending her party. The Haughton-Marshall and Ridgeley properties plaited their way across Dorset, throwing the two families together at every turn in the road. With the similarity in their ages, it was logical to conclude that Lady Oglesby and Lord Farling had known one another since they had been in leading strings.

The close, trapped feeling that Beth had experienced when her uncle had first insisted she must come to London had been considerably alleviated by her growing fondness for Jane, but the wires of Beth's cage seemed to appear again as another thought was forcibly brought to bear. No matter where she turned, she would be encountering her uncle's friends, and her every move would be remarked upon. Even though they made no deliberate attempt to assist him to monitor her every movement, his cronies would speak of having seen or met her, or that they had not had the pleasure. Even if she had meant to break her word, an action which her character would not accept with impunity, there was no way she could accomplish it without his learning of it.

It presently occurred to her that she might face a far greater danger from her uncle's close acquaintances than just the casual gossip among friends when a relative is mentioned. Since Lady Oglesby was more than likely a good friend of Lord Farling's, she could be in league with him to promote a romance between Beth and some gentleman she considered eligible. Beth shuddered, just thinking about it. She was aware, of course, that such things were often done, and were considered quite unexceptionable, but her father had never led her to believe he would make an arrangement for her, and the idea was repulsive. Just as odious was the thought that people she had never seen could be trying to arrange her life.

To enlist the aid of his friends was something Lord Farling would do, she knew, and the thought seemed to her like treachery. Suddenly she felt hounded—like the fox, trying to escape the baying pack.

The analogy gave her pause and she explored it carefully. The fox, with many adversaries, was often sly enough to outwit its enemies. It slipped through the fences, under the hedges, among the coverts and back to its den. The fox used the gaps in every obstruction to aid its flight. All she needed to do was find and use the openings between the restrictions her uncle had placed upon her.

Not even her most severe critic would have called Beth vain, but in Dorset she had been called particularly fetching, and the looks she had received that day from the Bond Street beaux were enough to show she would excite some interest on her own behalf. Added to that, the three highly productive properties in Dorset, along with a prudent father, had left her with a fortune not to be ignored. She had no expectations of taking the town by storm, but neither did she want the embarrassment of turning away prospective suitors in whom she had not the slightest interest. She was unable to imagine any gentleman in London going into raptures over breeding stock, well-drained fields, or a new strain of hens.

Still, none of it would signify if she could find the chink in her uncle's restrictions. It did occur to her that in order to escape its pursuers, the fox had to know its ground.

She leaned back against the confidante and smiled, her expression occasioning a wary question from Jane.

"My dear, that look is positively wicked. *What* are you thinking of?"

Beth's eyes flew wide as she sat up and leaned forward,

holding out her cup for a refill. "How can you say so, Jane? I was only thinking I must enjoy the party, and would not miss it for anything."

As Beth had no definite plan, further questioning by Jane elicited no more information. Beth was amused to see that along with her companion's frustration at not being privy to what she obviously thought was some outrageous scheme, there was in the little widow a suppressed enthusiasm. Beth wondered how her uncle could have been so wrong in his opinion of Jane Westcott.

Later, Beth retired to her apartment to don one of the acquisitions of the day, an aquamarine sarcenet. The over-skirt was a slightly darker shade and trimmed in the tiniest of emerald green ribbons. Beth had chosen her shawl, slippers, and reticule to match.

Ostrich feathers had long been out of fashion as part of a coiffure, so her purchase that day had occasioned remark by Jane, but that most amiable creature was unaware of the list of rules that had been placed on the young lady and the omissions that list contained. Lord Farling had not mentioned headgear or hair.

While Myra stood by, throwing her disapproving looks and chiding her for dawdling, Beth turned four brilliant green plumes in her hand, wondering what use she could make of them. She was seeking something different from the usual, something to set herself apart from the average young female in town to snare a husband. She tried holding them above her head, but her good taste would not condone that which was dowdy or passé. Instead she coaxed Myra into fashioning them into a cap that entwined beneath the titian curls and came down on the right to caress her cheek and slender white neck. Over the bright green, the red curls cascaded in long ringlets. She was not to realise until later that the effect was indeed breathtaking.

The official season had not yet begun, but there was a

crush in Lady Oglesby's salons. Beth suffered a momentary fright at her audacity with the ostrich feathers as she greeted her hostess. Every eye in the room seemed to be turned on her. It was not the first time she had encountered gentlemen with quizzing glasses, but to find numbers of those aids to vision leveled in her direction was daunting even to someone of her intrepid nature. The feeling that she was being inspected as if she were some rare specimen brought her head up and she fought to keep down the irritation.

It was apparent by the spare Egyptian motif of her rooms that Lady Oglesby was in the height of fashion, both in her wardrobe and her decor. Beth could not help the feeling of pleasure that invaded her as she admired the ceiling, which could hardly be less than an Adam design, but she pulled her eyes away, thinking it was hardly appropriate to stand around ogling the ceiling, with her mouth hanging open.

She transferred her attention to the guests, and was at once struck by the uniformity of clothing that automatically dropped them into clearly defined ranks. Those very young ladies who were in London for their first season shyly wore white and the very pale colours of the fledglings. The young ladies who were more than a year past their emergence from the schoolroom but still in the marriage mart had shed their paler plumage and opted for more colour. Beth, with both a sense of comfort and one of chagrin, realised she fitted in this group both in fact and in dress. She cast a wary eye at Jane Westcott, wondering if the widow had exercised more influence over her charge than Beth had realised.

It appeared to Beth as she looked out over the rooms that age was the factor that allowed the women of the *ton* to dress ever more brightly, until at a certain point the sobriety of dark colours and blacks held sway again. The dignities of the very dark shades were, it seemed, achieved with the status of sitting back, observing, remarking, and taking no part. There were a number of blackbirds on the fence, as Beth thought of them, watching as Jane Westcott did her duty by leading her around for introductions.

She wasn't to know until she had attended many other parties that Lady Oglesby was herself an eccentric of sorts. It was unusual at a rout party for the dancing to start so early and continue throughout the evening, but the hostess, with an enviable surfeit of rooms, had planned for the amusement of all her guests. Tables of whist were being organised in one small drawing room, while in the main salon the musicians had struck up a lively tune. In another a group of young people had begun a game of charades.

Beth would have preferred to stroll about with Jane Westcott, but the worthy chaperone, knowing her duty to Lord Farling, led her charge into the room where the music was drawing numbers of young people out onto the floor for a country dance.

As Beth looked over the room, she noticed there was a uniformity of rank in the clothing of the gentlemen also. It was not as readily apparent at first glance, since all were dressed in dark coats, black satin breeches, striped stockings, and slippers with buckles, but the differences were in the cuts of their coats, the vests, their neckcloths, and the heights of their collar points. Many of the younger men were affecting glorious concoctions below their chins and their collar points were so high as to make it impossible for them to turn their heads. Also, a number were wearing their jackets so tight that Beth wondered if they could do more than lift their arms the necessary amount to take their partners' hands. She restrained her smile and hoped they weren't thirsty during the evening, because surely they would never be able to raise a glass to their lips.

One such gentleman, standing alone, stared in a manner that Beth thought quite odiously rude. He had kept the ladies under inspection for some time before approaching them with an expression of extreme hauteur. She, with an almost involuntary reaction, straightened her already correct posture, feeling her inner hackles rise as he made a graceful affected leg to Jane.

"My dear lady, so good to see you again," he drawled. His overly cultured voice seemed to emanate from somewhere a foot in front of his face, as if he wore a mask and stood off behind it. "The last time was at Herversay, was it not? One does from time to time meet delightful people there, though it is often the most frightful bore to be invited, don't you agree?"

"Good evening, Lord Withington," Jane smiled tightly, and Beth gathered from the unaccustomed primness of her companion that the widow cared as little for the gentleman as Beth expected to. "I fear, if you are thinking of the ducal seat, you are mistaking me for someone else. I believe the last time I enjoyed the pleasure of your company was at Moreton."

When Jane denied the exalted company, the gentleman's eyebrows rose slightly, leaving the two ladies in no doubt that he had approached them with the expectation of finding them to be something more than they were. What their consequence was supposed to have been in order to satisfy the requirements of the viscount was not in the least clear. His condescending expression, once he lowered his brows, left them fully cognizant that they should be grateful that he was giving them the honour of his presence.

He pointedly turned to Beth. "I know, my dear one, that we have never met. Not even my wretched memory forgets both beauty and charm."

Beth smiled perfunctorily, making a polite remark as the dandy bowed over her hand, requesting the honour of leading her into the dance that was just forming.

They stood in an uncompleted set while he pointed out personalities, disparaging most and claiming a close acquaintance here and there, always accompanying his approval was a description of immense wealth or titles among the top ranks of the peerage.

"Who is the young lady in the divine white dress?" Beth asked. Her eye had been drawn to a small blonde who looked like a fairy princess.

"A provincial," Viscount Withington announced with loathing. "From some uncouth territory in India, I believe. If people *must* take their offspring to be raised totally without benefit of culture, I think it should behoove them not to foist those creatures back on the *ton*."

As long as Beth could remember, the little thrill that sprang from her toes and ran to her temples signalled danger—that inexorable danger that came from within when she determined on a course that usually collided head-on with discretion.

She dimpled and twinkled up at Lord Withington. "I quite know what you mean. India—a frightful place. For the life of me I cannot understand what anyone would see in it."

"Quite so," he replied haughtily.

"All that rain," Beth continued blithely. Monsoons came to mind, but that was all she could remember about that Eastern English possession. More readily to her mind leapt the details of the Arabian countries. She decided to impart some of that knowledge, sure she could overset his haughty demeanour.

"Personally I prefer a dryer climate. If one is going to leave England, it should be for a land that has some culture in its background. Now Arabia, in my opinion, is the place. The quaint customs have been around for unnumbered generations. When I lived there with my father, who is a noted archeologist, you know, I was so interested in the area. Don't you think it's lovely for everyone to eat out of a common bowl? Such a close spirit among those people."

"Oh—uh—quite," Lord Withington replied with a shudder. Her little speech had caused him to draw back as if he were partnering a cobra on the dance floor. Beth was unable to resist a parting shot.

"Yes, I thought so. Such a culture and such inventiveness. Do you know that on the desert, when they are far from where any wood may be obtained for the evening fires, they use camel—well, possibly we should not bring *that* into the conversation—" she let her words hang, biting her lips to prevent a smile as the viscount's eyes bulged.

"We should *not!*" Lord Withington answered in tones of purest revulsion and, as the dance was just ending, he led her back to Jane Westcott with all possible speed. Once he had bowed over Jane's hand and removed himself with a haste that was far from seemly, Jane turned to Beth, her eyebrows raised.

"Dear heavens," Jane murmured, looking from Beth to the rapidly retreating viscount. "What ever did you do to that man? He seemed positively frightened of you."

"I have no idea," Beth replied calmly. "We were discussing foreign travel."

"It's just as well." Jane opened her fan and fluttered it, allowing Beth to share the artificial breeze. "I own I cannot like the man. He is so puffed up in his own conceit that I find him a great bore. It's just as well if he does not form one of your court. Oh, dear—here comes another just as bad. It sounds terrible of me, I know, to appear as if I dislike everyone, but these airs of self consequence I cannot approve."

The Baron Arsvin was the second of several gentlemen who presented themselves for introduction and were what Jane, with an apology for her cant description, called the raff and scaff of the *ton*. Encouraged by her success in turning away Lord Withington, Beth listened to their slighting remarks until she discovered their particular weaknesses and gave her imagination full sway.

Her eyes sparkled with mischief as she watched the rotund baron hurry away, anxious to put as much distance as possible between himself and a young woman who shyly confessed that to keep up the family estates her parents had gone into trade. The Honourable John Sterns found greener pastures for his fortune hunting when she told him her estates were mortgaged to the hilt and she, too, was seeking an advantageous marriage. Lord Ithers, the third son of a marquis whose exalted name went right out of her head, though he mentioned it several times, took himself away when his raking boasts fell on the ears of a young lady who might possibly be bound for a convent.

Mr. Coster, a gentleman short in inches but long on a bored attitude, looked over his large, beaked nose at her as they took their places for the quadrille. He made conversation in a desultory manner that said he was far more interested in doing the pretty as fashion demanded than he was in her answers.

"I daresay, I have not seen you in London in years past," he remarked.

"No," Beth replied. "I usually find that one season interferes with the other."

"What other?" He looked slightly more interested.

"The fishing season," Beth was inspired to say. "I come from a long line of seafaring people, you know."

"Oh, yes, don't we all. Have a brother in the ships myself, but not in fishing."

"It's a living and puts food on the table," Beth replied as if she had answered the question a thousand times. "When we are short of help my sisters and I have to take out the boats." *There, that ought to do for him, and maybe now I can sit with Jane for a bit,* she thought, but she had reckoned without her partner. Suddenly all his air of boredom was forgotten as he gazed at her, fascinated.

"Do you really? That's something, it is that! Have you ever been out in a storm?"

Beth missed her step as she stared at him, startled. Was he

quizzing her, she wondered? Hadn't anyone told him fishing was not a fit subject within *ton*nish circles? No, he had caught on to her game and was planning on giving her her own back again, she decided. Well, he was going to find that a bit more difficult than he supposed. She armed herself with a bored expression.

"Everyone asks that," she answered casually. "What else can you expect in the North Sea?"

"Really? Must be quite dangerous, I'd say. Waves get very high?"

"Oh, not above sixty or seventy feet." Beth threw out the figures with abandon, wondering what they meant in actual size. Apart from his deplorable tendency to say "really," he was holding up his end of the game admirably. She determined in future to be more careful about mistaking an unprepossessing appearance for dull-wittedness. Determined not to lose by default, she dredged her memory for the details of a very lively book she had found in her father's library in Carthalin Hall. It was amazing how much of the story stuck in her memory after Aunt Sarah had whisked it away, saying it was something no young lady of sensibility should read.

At his insistence, she gave him a rising account of a storm at sea, even including being washed overboard. Hoping she could prevent him from asking how she regained the ship, she finished breathlessly, saying she hoped she never went through that experience again.

They had both been intent on her tale and a misstep caused Beth to turn her heel. As a final touch, or so she thought, to add veracity to her statements, she quietly ejaculated the expletive used by the main character in the book.

"Whale's tails!"

Mr. Coster's eyes bugged out. "Really! That's a dashed strange thing to fish for! Why not the entire whale?"

Too late she realised he had been asking her a question, and had taken the expletive to be the answer. *Well,* she thought with resignation, *in for a penny, in for a pound.* She put her imagination to work again. Lifting her chin and adopting a very superior tone of voice, she explained with an air of patience, "Because we don't need the entire whale, you see. We just chop off the tail and throw the creature back. They immediately grow new ones. Earthworms and a lot of sea creatures do that, you know." She took a deep breath and wondered if the dance would never end. There was nothing left to do but put the crown on her ridiculous story. "One creature has had her tail removed so often I've named her. I call her Agatha."

Sure that had to bring out his hidden amusement, she gazed up at him and was astonished to see the pallour of his face. Her heart came up into her throat. He could hide his amusement, but no one could go pale at will. He believed every word!

Suddenly she couldn't continue with the farce. Her mouth went as dry as her brain. With heartfelt gratitude she heard the last note of the musicians and suggested he take her back to Jane. Unlike her other partners, he was not disposed to rush, and it was Beth who had to hurry him across the floor. On the way she kept up a disjointed running chatter to forestall more inquiry.

"Dear Jane," she said as she reached her chaperone. "Isn't that the dear lady you wanted to introduce me to?" Beth pointed to a woman just heading for the parlour that held the whist tables. She gripped Jane's arm, giving her a nudge in that direction.

"Oh, but I say, I do want to talk about your experiences at greater length," Mr. Coster protested.

"We will," Beth smiled brightly. "I'll rejoin you as soon as I can. Do come along, Jane."

"Dear, you do have the most singular effect on people," Jane complained as they hurried away.

"Never mind that, just get me out of here," Beth replied.

To Beth's profound relief, they became engaged in conversation with a long-winded matron who kept them at her side until Jane begged off, pleading another party that they had promised to look in on. Mr. Coster, clearly hopeful of continuing the conversation, lingered in the background until the sight of a pair of black-clad shoulders threw Beth into a case of the fidgets.

Jane, at every possible opportunity, gave her companion questioning looks, and when they had at last made their escape, ventured to inquire what had put Beth in such a taking, but she was not to get a satisfactory answer. While the widow might be amenable to omitting a few social functions, she was still answerable to Lord Farling, and could not be expected to aid or even condone a plan to deliberately turn away prospective suitors.

For the next two days, inclement weather made it exceedingly uncomfortable to shop or visit, so Beth and Jane spent a quiet time before a cozy fire. Jane busied herself with her embroidery and, after asking Beth if she had a desire to travel, allowed the young lady an uninterrupted study of the guide book. Encouraged by the response of most of her partners, and rapidly getting over her nervousness about the tale she had told Mr. Coster, she was arming herself to drive away the rest of the "raff and scaff." She had, however, made up her mind to be very sure about the people to whom she told her tales. The last thing she needed was another Mr. Coster.

Late in the second afternoon, a travel-stained coach arrived and Hughes announced Lord Farling. Despite the bad weather, he entered the drawing room impeccably attired, looking as fresh as if he had just left his valet. He informed them that he left Carlsbury Manor earlier that afternoon and would join them for dinner before going on to his club.

"And how are you enjoying London?" he asked Beth as he bowed over her hand.

"You know where I *want* to be," she answered quietly. "Did you stop by Carthalin Hall on your way to town? How was Lady Anne?"

"I did stop before leaving home," he replied. "She was doing fine—her colts are feisty little fellows. You will have two of the finest hunters in the country in a couple of years." His eyes twinkled as he gazed at his niece. "You see, I am taking my task seriously, as I hope you are yours." Still holding her hand, he turned her about, viewing her morning dress with a raised quizzing glass. "Charming, and in the first style of fashion. I couldn't ask for anything more fitting. Have you started going out into society?"

Beth told him about the rout party, saying only that she had attended and enjoyed it, leaving it to Jane to give a fuller description of the entertainment and whom they had met.

Beth sat back and watched the two old friends in conversation. Jane, always a lively person, was at once both heightened in colour and more demure as she answered Lord Farling's questions. For once her interminable embroidery was laid aside, and she sat with folded hands, giving her attention to Beth's uncle.

By the time dinner was announced they had exhausted the current gossip and had regressed to tales of when they had been on the town as youths. Their conversation held nothing of interest for Beth and, since they were deeply involved, she tried to concentrate on the buttered lobsters and the green goose that constituted to her the most delectable part of the second course.

When they left the dining room, they bade Lord Farling good evening, because he still held to his plan of retiring to his club for a game of whist.

*   *   *

Breakfast was a surprise for both ladies.

When Beth entered the small dining parlour she found her uncle already busy with a sirloin and buttered eggs. His expression when he looked up at her was lacking all the cheerfulness of the previous evening. Not even Jane's entrance served to lighten the air of gravity that he had laid over the room.

While Jane poured chocolate for herself and Beth, the younger lady chose an egg and a kipper from the sideboard.

"Are you sure you're eating enough?" Lord Farling asked coldly.

"I beg your pardon?" Beth looked up, surprised. "I think so. It would be shameful of me to put on weight and not be able to wear my new wardrobe."

"But is it sustaining? Or possibly I am amiss in worrying. Could it be that this is not your day for fishing in the North Sea? You do have a busy schedule, I know."

Jane, who had been spreading a piece of toast with marmalade, turned to gaze at the gentleman with lively astonishment.

"Gubby, whatever can you mean? Surely Beth has no such intention. Even if she did it would take days to reach it, so what would today's breakfast say to anything?"

"Well, if she doesn't care for that, she could dig up old bones in Arabia and dip her fingers in the common bowl," Lord Farling replied with suppressed rage. "Or maybe a shop girl will not appear and she must wait on customers?"

Jane looked more confused than ever, but then a thought struck her, causing her to narrow her eyes. "Gubby, far be it from me to criticise, but was the port especially good last evening?"

"I'm *not* bosky!" Lord Farling snapped. "Young lady, you gave me your word! To behave in a manner fitting—"

"Oh, no!" Beth replied archly. She had been confused at

35

first by her uncle's tirade, but she sat through the rest with growing humour. "That was not the agreement. I remember every word. I promised to behave with civility and charm. I assure you, Uncle, I told those stories with both ·civility and all the charm with which you credited me."

Lord Farling lost his temper. "Am I going to have to set a new rule every day?" he roared, slamming the table until the cups rattled.

"No." Beth smiled wickedly. "Because you cannot! If you remember, you gave me your word that there would be no more restrictions. And lay none of the blame on Jane, because she knew nothing of it and couldn't have stopped me if she had."

Across the breakfast table the uncle and niece eyed each other. Jane sat ignoring her breakfast, apparently not daring to move for fear the two implacable characters would turn on her.

Suddenly Lord Farling rose from the table, saying he was taking his coffee in the book room. He stomped through the door and out of sight.

Jane looked at Beth with an expression of awe. "I cannot believe you really did it!"

"Do believe it, Jane. Don't look so thunderstruck. It was the most diverting thing imaginable. I only had one bad moment, and that was when Mr. Coster insisted I continue the tale about the North Sea. Do you think the waves could get sixty feet high?"

Jane looked thoughtful for a moment and then smiled. "I have no idea, dearest, but I'll wager a hundred guineas that Mr. Coster doesn't know either. Now *do* go shopping and let me see if I can calm your uncle."

With Beth safely out of the house, Jane arranged a tray with coffee and two cups. A footman carried it into the book room and she entered just after he came out. Lord Farling frowned up at her as she poured the coffee.

"Lord, Jane, how could you let that dratted girl cut such a caper?"

Jane handed him his coffee and settled in a chair by the crackling fire. "I didn't know about it," she replied meekly. "But if I had, how was I, or even you, to stop her? She's not a child."

"Well, when I hired you, I expected you to exercise some control over her."

Jane bowed her head. "I do try, but if you won't be offended, I must tell you, shouting at her will only put her back up and cause her to do something even more outrageous. I'm convinced, Gubby, that she has a good head on her shoulders, she's gently born and bred, and her good taste will reassert itself in time to keep her from doing anything too drastic. I believe—if she's not pushed too hard—she'll let her basic good taste rule. And what harm has been done? There was only one of her dancing partners at the Oglesby house that you would have considered eligible. From what she told me, he was not at all offended. I am persuaded the *ton* will not ostracise her for quizzing several obnoxious and gazetted fortune hunters."

Lord Farling leaned back in his chair and smiled.

"You're right, my dear. Far from getting the reputation of being a penniless shopkeeper's daughter, she's credited with being a very sharp and discerning wit. The whole of White's is laughing about it. Sorry I missed it when that sharp-tongued Withington started sneering at her for eating out of a common bowl in Arabia, only to have Jackson insist it was a lie, that she had followed her father's troop through the Pyrenees, and Ithers saying she'd been a nun or some such. Lord, what a dust they say it was, and there was Coster, yapping about the North Sea. Do they really cut the tails off whales?"

Jane shook her head. "I'm sure I don't know, Gubby, but

this worries me exceedingly. I hope she hasn't been too clever for her own good."

Lord Farling leaned back chuckling. "Oh, but she has, Jane, she has. Instead of being ostracised, and I think that was her intention, she's made herself the rage. Tighten your cinch, old girl, you're in for a busy season."

= 3 =

LORD FARLING REMAINED in the house for the rest of the day, discussing his investments with his London man of business, and when Beth returned from her shopping, she, too, was drawn into the book room. The afternoon dragged on until tea as she listened to a long, boring account of her own investments, something she would have preferred to see on paper to study carefully, but her uncle was anxious she should have a detailed accounting.

That evening he took the two ladies to the theatre, and so it was not until the next morning after he had left for another visit out of town that Beth and Jane were able to have a tête-a-tête.

Frustration, anger, and more than a little disbelief showed in Beth's face as she opened the stack of invitations that had arrived in the early morning post.

"I don't understand what happened," she cried.

Jane, who had just entered the drawing room, took a seat on the sofa by the window and sorted through the buff coloured cards.

"It *is* tedious to have one's plans overset with such a complete reversal," Jane sympathised. "From the way Gubby explained it to me, the *ton* think you deliberately gave setdowns to their most unpopular members. They do love one who will do their dirty work. Forgive me for sliding from the purpose, but isn't it interesting that Mr. Coster, a truly estimable young man, was among that number, and because he did not consider himself insulted, no one else did?''

"No—yes—oh, I don't know.'' Beth dropped the rest of the invitations on the cushions next to Jane and threw herself into a chair. "It wasn't my intention to cut anyone—no, that's not true at all.'' The baleful look she gave Jane changed to a rueful smile. "I did enjoy putting both Lord Withington and Baron Arsvin out of countenance. Odious. One as bad as the other. But who would have expected this?'' she flicked a hand at the invitations. "It means starting all over—now I have to—'' She lapsed into silence.

"You have to what, dear?''

"Oh, nothing,'' Beth answered carelessly. She thought it unwise to tell Jane in forthright terms that she was even then searching for another way to circumvent her uncle's plans so she could return to her farms.

Just then they were interrupted by a discreet knock and Hughes announced the Marquis of Alspeth. Beth was aware that the gentleman was Jane's nephew, and her surprise was tinged with a slight irritation, thinking Jane was attempting to be a matchmaker. A sharp look at her companion caused her to doubt it, however. The widow's mouth flew open in surprise and she dropped her embroidery in her confusion as she rose to greet him.

"My dear Steven! I had no idea you were in London!''

Beth watched as the gentleman made his leg to his aunt. He was singularly graceful for one of his height. By the snowy whiteness of his starched linen, the flattering disarray of his hair done *à la Brutus,* and the gleam of his Hessians, she had little doubt he was the epitome of fashion. Any ideas to the contrary were quickly dispelled when his left hand showed an enamelled snuff box and a lace-trimmed handkerchief held nonchalantly in the crook of his little finger. He was elegantly slim, yet the excellent cut of his coat and pantaloons displayed to advantage his well-formed muscles. A singularly strong profile softened as he smiled at his aunt.

"I've been in town for a few days," he said, as with a casual flick of the lace handkerchief he indicated his clothing. "But only a delivery from Weston's would allow me to show my face. It's a bore, returning to town after two year's absence and finding oneself completely out of fashion. Then I think of having to face a tailor with their tapes and pins and I'm ready to leave immediately."

Jane smiled up at him. "You must let Lady Beth instruct you on how such things are arranged. Dear me! I must be growing witless, lacking in all manners. Lady Elizabeth Haughton-Marshall, my nephew and dearest relative, Steven Hepsford, the Marquis of Alspeth."

As the marquis stepped forward to acknowledge the introduction, Beth discovered he was even taller than she first thought. While he was greeting his aunt his words, combined with his profile, had made him appear haughty, but when he turned his attention to Beth, she saw the humour in his dark, handsome face.

"Your servant," he said as he bowed over her hand. Upon straightening, he turned toward the door. "Well, don't just stand there, Puppy. Get in here and make your bow to the ladies."

It was then that Lady Beth saw the very young man in the doorway. As he came shyly forward she noticed he was nearly as tall as the marquis, though his youthful frame still had the ranginess of new growth. He would hardly be more than eighteen years old. His clothing was as elegant as that of the marquis, but he suffered from an acute discomfort and was totally lacking in poise.

Lord Alspeth introduced him to Jane in an offhand manner. "One of Fred's offshoots. Seems I'm to do something with him. Thank God he's the last of that graceless litter."

The young Mr. Jonathan Thorpe, when introduced to his hostess, was all stammer and blush. He quickly retired to a chair, sitting with his hands clasped nervously around his knees.

The marquis turned back to Beth. "I'm intensely interested in what my aunt said. Have you some mysterious way of getting around tailors and their interminable chalks and pins?"

Beth picked up the handkerchief that she was labouriously trying to hem with tiny stitches. She knew Jane had been referring to her successful attempt at sidestepping numerous fittings by sending her maid to stand in for her. Still the humourous quirk in her nature caused her to answer the marquis's question literally.

"Well, I can safely say that I have spent very little time in the engaging company of tailors. As a matter of fact, Weston's has given me no trouble at all."

The marquis nodded approvingly. "Touché, and if sprigged muslin looked as well on my person, I, too, would forgo them, but alas, I fear I have not the complexion for it."

Jane laughed and looked delighted with the conversation. "Truly, Steven, I have so missed your company. It is marvelous to hear your droll wit again."

"Oh, we had hoped you would be staying with us as Uncle Steven's hostess—" At a glare from the marquis, young Mr. Thorpe bit his bottom lip and flushed a bright crimson.

The uncomfortable silence that followed was broken by Jane, who only briefly glanced up from her embroidery. "I am gratified that you thought of me, but I am convinced that Martha will undertake the task for you and do it splendidly. I find that Lady Beth and I suit very well."

"Oh, Jane, I am quite undone." Beth let the unfinished handkerchief fall to her lap. "If you are needed by your family—"

"I'm not, dearest Beth. It would not do at all for me to be

42

Steven's hostess. I'm far too absentminded and would most assuredly forget to order half the dinner or some such. The only reason he wants me is because he knows I will not prate at him over his foolish schemes for entertainment. Martha will be much better at running his house—she might even keep him in hand." The widow went placidly on with the intricate stitching.

"But—" Beth's protestations were cut short by the marquis.

"Don't fret yourself, Lady Beth. Everything my aunt says is true, you know." He leaned back in his chair and took a pinch of snuff. "I shudder to think what my comfort would be like with her as hostess. In fact, it serves my purposes better to have Aunt Martha run my household—but she is *such* a missish bore. In return for whisking my favourite relative away, however, you must give me leave to visit her often. She is the only thing that makes my hodge-podge of a family bearable."

"Of course, you must come whenever you choose," Beth insisted, still feeling vaguely guilty.

"Careful, my lady, I will take you at your word. May I, in fact, invite the two of you to drive out with me tomorrow? Say, at one?"

"Oh, I should like that!" Jane blurted out and then turned an anxious look upon her charge. "You voiced your desire to purchase a town carriage. Longacre is the only place to go, but it would be much better if we had the company of a gentleman."

Jane's hopeful look was so much like a child's that Beth could not resist teasing her. "My lord just told us he dislikes shopping. After stealing away his favourite aunt, I am convinced it would be odious of me to lay upon him the displeasing task of kicking his heels while I choose a carriage."

"My lady, you wrong me. It's pins and chalk I abhor," the

marquis objected. "Longacre happens to be on my own list of most urgent business. My town stables are sadly lacking in modern equipage. While you select a town carriage, I will be busy with something more in the sporting line."

"Then I most gratefully accept your invitation," Beth replied with a smile.

As the gentlemen prepared to depart, Beth watched the marquis under her lashes. She appreciated his wit but wondered about the faint air of boredom. He didn't seem to be trying to fix her attentions, she noticed, which made him at once more attractive as a companion and irritating to her pride. She did like the warmth he showed to Jane, proving his very real affection for his aunt.

The next morning, as she prepared for her drive, Beth was again thinking about the marquis. It was, therefore, with some shock that she received Myra's comment.

"I do declare, you are really doing it up fine today."

Beth deposited her brush on the dressing table with an impatient clatter. "It would be a fine thing for my farms if I did not!" she snapped. With a few hasty pats at her curls she sailed out of the room.

Precisely at one Lord Alspeth arrived in a barouche complete with driver. In consideration of his horses, the ladies were ready, and after a few civilities were exchanged in the drawing room they were on their way to Longacre.

The day was brisk and fair, and a number of people were strolling on Conduit Street. Many raised their hands in salutation as the carriage passed.

Lord Alspeth, sitting with his back to the driver, was facing the ladies. As they turned into Regent's Street, he leaned toward Beth.

"Have you decided what type of carriage would suit you?" The question was on the surface innocent, but the twinkle in his eye put Beth on the alert.

"I thought it best to see what was offered before I made

my decision," she said cautiously.

The marquis sat back in his seat and gazed into the distance. "I just thought you might have some specific purpose in mind, such as in addition to social events, you might be interested in transporting nuns or trade goods."

"Steven! Not you too!" Jane gave a sudden plump of her skirts as she pouted and looked more than ever like a setting hen. "I am persuaded everyone in London has heard of Beth's—taradiddles? Is that right? I do feel quite left out. I must think they were quite diverting, else there should not be so much talk."

Beth pursed her lips to keep away the smile that threatened her composure. "There is some merit in what you suggest." She nodded thoughtfully at the marquis. "When we're not shopping or going to balls, I could use the carriage for transporting fish."

"Fish?" Jane looked astonished.

"More precisely, whales' tails," said the marquis, whereupon Jane threw up her hands and rolled her eyes in the manner of a broad comedy actress as she entered the spirit of the discussion.

The marquis leaned back, folded his arms, and gazed at Beth with tolerant amusement.

"Now, that was a story that interested me greatly. Mr. Coster was quite taken with it—even when he learned it was a quiz he was fascinated. Are you aware that your adventures were very similar to those in Mr. Gordon White's book, *The Monster in the Sea*? Of course, it is a coincidence. It is far too warm a book for a lady to read—still, I was struck with the similarity. Especially the time the cargo lashed to the deck broke loose and knocked you overboard. I wonder how *you* escaped your peril."

Beth's eyes widened. "Why, in the only way possible, sir. I drowned."

Lord Alspeth's laughter delayed them from leaving the

barouche, as they had just at that moment pulled up in front of the cavernous warehouses of Longacre.

Beth had expected the marquis to leave them with the manager, but he walked with Jane as Beth inspected and rejected several elegant vehicles that would be suitable for social engagements. The manager kept up a flow of running talk, describing all the features of the various town carriages, and Beth vouchsafed few answers. Therefore, everyone seemed quite surprised at her choice.

"I would like *that* body put on this undercarriage and the shaft modified for a team," she said with decision. "You will, of course, charge me for the alterations and make delivery as soon as possible."

While the manager looked thunderstruck, the marquis crossed his arms over his chest and raised his eyebrows, nodding his approval. "Excellent choice."

Beth looked up calmly. "Like you, sir, I have no wish to be seen at a disadvantage, but I will not risk losing a wheel and being tossed on the pavement if the team happens to take exception to a bright parasol." She pointed to the too slender wheels of the elegant vehicle that held the chosen body. "One strike against the curbing and that would be the result. Now, I believe sporting vehicles were next on the list."

"If you will not be bored." The marquis bowed.

"I assure you, sir, I will not."

The marquis was to receive his second surprise as they walked among the high-perch phaetons. Since the season had only just begun the influx of the polite society was just beginning. In anticipation of a demand for sporting vehicles, the warehouse offered an impressive choice. As they walked about, looking at the various styles, both the marquis and Beth came to a halt at the same time. They stood looking at a singularly graceful high-perch phaeton, the seat some five feet above the ground, the rear wheels very much larger than was the current fashion. The seat was contoured to fit the driver and passenger, and above it the actual back rest and ornamental frame flared out with the grace of wings. It was altogether the most elegant vehicle in the place, and in addition, the undercarriage was both strongly and lightly built.

"I'd like that one," Beth said with decision.

"I'll take it," the marquis announced at the same time.

They turned to each other in surprise. Lord Alspeth inclined his head as if making a bow.

"I know it would be good manners to give way to your desires, my lady, but are you sure you *want* such a vehicle?"

She mimicked his mock bow. "Quite sure, my lord, but you must *not* give way simply because I am a female. Since it is after all, a sporting vehicle, you must have a sporting chance. Shall we have the manager hold it for us and settle the issue, say, with a game of whist?"

What the marquis's answer might have been Beth was not to learn, because the manager, all smiles and bows, cried, "There is no need—indeed I have two, and the other is just a bit farther on. One has brown upholstery and the other green. That's the only difference."

Beth smiled on her companions. "Then we will allow my lord to make his choice. I plan to repaint and reupholster mine in any case, and the shaft must again be altered."

Lord Alspeth affected to shock. "I trust m'dear, that with your excellent eye for vehicles, you will not do anything so drastic as to have it painted pink?"

"Sir, how did you know?"

"White!" Jane announced decisively. She had been trailing the two shoppers and until then had remained completely silent, so her emphatic statement drew their startled attention.

"The undercarriage and the body shall be white with small but intricate black tracing—nothing so missish as flowers or any other recognisable design." While she had been speaking, she had marched around both the marquis and Beth. She nimbly climbed the steps, seating herself on the passenger side of the phaeton, and looked down at them.

"The upholstery shall be white velvet, and you shall have several white driving outfits made. On those occasions I will wear something pale so as not to detract from the picture you will make. Other times you will be dressed in vibrant colours. My, but you will be a vision, dearest." She bounced lightly, testing the springs, and looked very content on her elevated seat.

"My God!" The marquis looked up at his aunt with awe. "I always knew you were a right one, Jane, but I never thought to see you become a racing woman."

"But Steven, dear, there has been nothing said about racing. You know perfectly well that Beth cannot drive alone."

As she held her hands out to him for assistance, the marquis helped her to the floor of the warehouse and stood grinning down at her.

"It is customary for a tiger to accompany the driver of a phaeton, Aunt."

Jane adjusted her bonnet and twitched her skirts in place.

"Since I am persuaded that it will not serve for a male to accompany Lady Beth, I shall have to learn to roar."

=4=

BACK IN BERKELEY Square, Beth waited until the tea tray had been carried into the drawing room and the door had closed behind Hughes. Then she spoke what was on her mind.

"Jane, I am undone. You can't know the horrors that I envisioned when I first learned I was to have a hired chaperone in London, and how delighted I am that you and I suit so well. Nothing would induce me to be so unfeeling as to put you to the slightest discomfort, else you might leave me and I might get the creature of my imaginings. I have a very good reason for wanting the phaeton, but I would rather forgo it than have you feel you must accompany me. It will be quite unexceptionable for me to have a groom in attendance, especially Omes, who has been with the family for years and is quite up in age."

Jane laid aside her needlework and looked up at Beth petulantly. "You would not be cruel enough to leave me behind. I am *so* looking forward to it—and Omes will not do. He is *not* so advanced in years that it would be proper for you to refuse to put him down, should some gentleman opportune you for a turn about the park. However, it would not be the thing at all for you to leave me to walk by myself."

Beth gave out with a laugh that would have frightened her hens into a fortnight of infertility. "My uncle would consider you quite disloyal."

Jane smiled and picked up her needle again. "I'm sure

of that, but he forgets that I, too, once had overbearing relatives, you see."

"Then you know how I am placed!" Beth reached for a second piece of bread and butter, finding her appetite much better than it had been for days.

"How could I not, when I was expressly ordered to see that nothing was placed in the way of finding you a suitable match, and even more stringently instructed to keep you from preventing it. Now, my dear, *why* would you wish to prevent something you *wanted*? I doubt that I will ever understand a preference for chickens and livestock over gentlemen, but allow you the choice, I will."

"Not all chickens, dear Jane. Only certain ones and for certain purposes."

Jane gazed at the fire, pointedly avoiding Beth's eyes. "But have you considered that the same might hold true of gentlemen? Would it be in your best interest to injure yourself by turning away the one who laid claim upon your heart?"

"I suppose not," Beth sighed, "but to be that one, the gentleman must accept my chickens or I shall not accept him. Stop laughing at me Jane, I'm serious. I am persuaded that the social life will not do for me. I'll never be content to sit in a drawing room day after day and busy my head with clothing, dancing, morning visits, and games of loo. To me it would be—it already is a bore."

"Well, I am glad we had this talk," Jane said as she frowned over her French knots. "I will now know how to proceed. It will be my duty to discover among your eligible acquaintances which gentlemen know the productivity of their hen houses, and we will discount all those who do not."

So saying, she carefully put aside her embroidery and removed from the sewing basket a packet of buff envelopes containing invitations. A few fell to the floor.

"Tedious as you may find it, my dear, there is no hope for

it now. We must make some decisions about our social engagements."

Beth eyed her doubtfully and reached to pick up several of the dropped invitations. As she gathered them, she noticed two lists.

"What are these?" she asked as she recognised some well-known names.

Jane took the lists from her hand, scanned them and made a face as she handed them back. "That compilation of names is my suggestion for morning visits. I thought at first we would begin with the least boring of our relatives."

"And these?" Lady Beth raised her brows at the impressive list.

"Those we must not offend, and will therefore avoid, if possible," Jane Westcott remarked in a matter-of-fact voice as she thumbed through several cards. "Of course we cannot avoid them all—ah, here it is. Our voucher for Almack's. Tomorrow night we *must* put in our appearance. It will not do to ignore the worthy hostesses of the most celebrated salon in the polite world. Though, my dear, it is surely dreary in comparison with many. I do dislike orgeat excessively, and the table stakes! You chance to win or lose more playing in the schoolroom." She sighed. "It would bring your uncle down on our heads, however, if we should not go."

Lady Beth laughed. "I do declare, you quite put me in mind to have some relative escort me rather than put you to the trouble. I beg you will remember I am the one who is supposed to do the objecting. Quite seriously, Jane, do you dislike it really, or is this a ruse to make me less dissatisfied with my lot?"

Mrs. Westcott looked thoughtful. "Now, how must I answer that? I am not at all anxious to spend my evening there among the dowagers, no. But still it is truly better than companioning some monstrous old crone or acting as a governess, and that would be my alternative." At Lady Beth's surprise she reached over and patted the younger woman's hand. "The terrible truth, my love, is that I have not been as careful of my competence as I should have. I know I could apply to my nephew, and he would be the soul of generosity, but I am convinced I should not like that. I, too, am independent, you know. This task pleases me very well, your uncle is generous with what he pays me, and I am most certain that no one could be more suited to you than me."

"On that, dear Jane, we are in total agreement." Beth clasped the hand that was laid upon hers. "You are the one very bright spot in my trip to London."

Just then the footman entered, inquiring if the ladies were at home to Mr. Jonathan Thorpe.

Beth was thankful she answered in the affirmative, because the young man, instead of waiting in the entrance hall, had followed close on the heels of the servant and entered the room just as the footman was receiving word to show him in. Jonny was oblivious to the affronted servant as he came forward to make an awkward leg to Beth and his great-aunt.

"Thought I would find Uncle Steven here," he explained, with little veracity in his voice.

"No, I'm afraid you've missed him, dear," Jane replied.

"We're just having tea," Beth said, reaching for another cup and saucer. "Will you have a cup?"

"Oh, no, I should be imposing," he said, his expression so hopeful of his presence being urged that Beth repressed her smile with difficulty while she implored him to stay.

Stepping into the hall, she sent orders to the kitchen that a young gentleman with a large appetite was shortly going to deplete the small store of buttered bread and cakes left on the tray.

Jane kept up a running conversation with Jonny, and as Beth re-entered the room she heard him mention meeting Viscount Rathsham and his family. There was a feigned nonchalance, a certain offhand manner, followed by a hopeful silence, that alerted her. Beth, as an only child, was not used to having brothers about the house, but she had seen the servants and the sons of her tenant farmers in the throes of first love. Often she had silently suffered along with them. Jane, for all her perspicacity, had not noticed the all-important clue to Jonny's reason for the visit.

"Viscount Rathsham—" Beth mused aloud. "I wonder— do I know of them? The name sounds familiar—he could have been a friend of my father's—" She let the idea trail off, trusting Jonny to pick up on it immediately.

"I should say he might!" The young man brightened, suddenly all eagerness. "If you could find time to leave a card, I daresay Lady Rathsham would appreciate it. Newly arrived in town, you know."

While Jane might have missed Jonny's original overtures to the ladies to assist in his newest, if not his first, love affair, she was by no means obtuse.

"We could invite them to tea?" She turned inquiring eyes on Lady Beth, making her suggestion into a question.

"An excellent idea," Beth nodded. "I do think, though, that we should also solicit the presence of Mr. Thorpe and Lord Alspeth if they would be so good as to give us their time."

"And well we might!" Jonny agreed readily. "At least, I can speak for myself, and Uncle Steven would probably like to come. You can depend on me for anything," he enthusiastically informed Beth, and then coloured under what he obviously thought she might consider an impertinence on his part.

Beth, however, had heard the words that at the moment were most welcome. Before Jonny's blush reached his eyes, she was accepting his offer.

"That statement, sir, you may rue. What I miss most is not being able to ride, and some perversity of character prevents me from taking a groom as company. I detest the thought, as though I was either still in leading strings, or needed protection. Still, even more I dislike having my horses in town, getting their only exercise from my employees, while I am prevented from one of my chief pleasures. If you would care to accompany me in the park tomorrow morning, I would be glad to provide a mount.''

Jonny was perched on the edge of his chair, the discomfort he suffered forgotten entirely. ''Lady Beth, you are a real out-and-outer! Most of the time, when a female wants a fellow to do something for her, it's some silly thing like getting her shawl or her reticule or going to some boring party or another. I've been hoping to find someone to ride in the park in the mornings. It's no good at all, going by one's self.''

''I'm so glad we are in sympathy,'' Beth laughed at his artless admission, ''and I'll try to maintain my reputation for being an out-and-outer by never asking you to a dull party, or having you fetch anything.''

''Oh, I'd come to the dullest party for you,'' Jonny said reverently, still unaware of his gauche remark. ''Uncle Steven brought a bit of blood and bone to town for my use. I'll be here in the morning, never fear.''

With those words he gulped down the rest of his tea, stuffed half a scone in his mouth, took another in his hand, and made a sketchy bow to both ladies before hurtling through the door.

''I must speak to Steven.'' Jane stared at the offending open door with disapproval. ''Jonny's manners are deplorable. He must learn to do his duty by his hostess.''

Beth laughed and crossed the room to close the door. ''His manners are perfect for a young man who is both in love and about to be seen in the park on a bit of blood and bone, Jane. What would you have him? A youth without spirit?''

The next morning, Jonny's arrival at the door of Berkeley

54

Square coincided exactly with that of the two grooms who led a pale grey stallion of uncertain temperament.

Beth, dressed in a blue riding habit with gold braiding on the cuffs of her jacket and adorning the matching hat, descended the steps.

"Good morning, Jonny. I hope you are in the mood for a good ride."

"I am," the young man answered absently as he watched the restive brute, barely held in check by a groom's full weight on the bridle. "You aren't going to ride *that* animal, are you?"

"Storm? Why, of course!" Beth gave the boy a gaze that showed her astonishment. "Being deprived of riding him has been a blight on my stay in London."

While Jonny watched dubiously, and the first groom held tightly to the reins, the second gave Beth a hand and threw her into the saddle.

"Give him a minute to settle down," Beth called to Jonny as the first groom freed the bridle. There ensued a confusion while the grooms scampered out of the path of the stallion, who reared, sidled, and in general behaved like anything but a well-mannered riding horse, causing Jonny's mount to react nervously.

To his chagrin, both stablemen completely ignored their mistress as she held her seat upon the plunging grey and acted as if they meant to assist him. With a harder hand than he was accustomed to using, Jonny brought his animal out of its capriciousness and made an effort to catch the bridle of the grey.

Seeing his intent, Beth laughed and exercised her own reins, turning the grey in the opposite direction. "Give him a moment," she repeated, completely at ease on the skittish horse. "Remember, he's been shut up in a town stable, and he likes it no better than I do—but that's enough, Storm. If you want a run, calm down—that's the boy."

With a firm hand on the reins she quieted the spirited mount and turned his head in the direction of Hyde Park. With Jonny riding at her side, warily eyeing her horse, they entered the park behind Ashly Place and turned down Rotten Row. Because of the early hour, no other riders were in sight.

"I know we're not supposed to gallop here, but I'd love to let Storm stretch his legs," Beth said to Jonny, whose frown had deepened as the stallion showed no disposition to settle down. The mount was still sidling back and forth across the path, and Beth allowed him his play, only pulling him in when she wished to speak to her companion.

"Not the thing," Jonny shook his head. "Not supposed to gallop in Hyde Park, Uncle Steven says." If he was paying more that the usual amount of attention to the strictures of Lord Alspeth, justification presented itself as he eyed Storm.

"Who's to see?" Beth returned. "But if you are in danger of your uncle's anger, then don't accompany me." She eased off on the reins and Storm leapt off for the coveted gallop.

"Now, see here!" Jonny's shout reached her and she could hear the hoofbeats of his mount as he gave chase, but his horse, she knew, would not be able to catch or even pace the grey stallion.

As she rounded a turn in the path she cast a quick glance over her shoulder to see Jonny making a desperate try. Thinking it would do no harm for him to put his uncle's horse through its paces, she let Storm lengthen his stride.

Flying along the bridle path brought back all the happiness of life at Carthalin Hall. The pale grey horse was associated with all the memories of the girlhood spent in those fertile fields. She could still picture Storm as a gangly colt, running at his dam's side while Beth rode the mare. Her stablemen had objected, accusing her of outrageously spoiling the young stallion. She still did, she knew, but the eagerness she felt through the reins was infectious.

Not until she had reached the western end of the park did she slacken her pace and subdue the stallion to a prancing walk. Then doubt assailed her. She had given Jonny a reasonable time to come up with her, but there was no sign of the boy. Reversing her direction, she cantered back down the path, and near the center of the park she came upon Jonny, leading his limping mount. Beth slid from the saddle and dropped lightly to the ground.

"Jonny! What happened?"

"Don't quite know," he said quietly, not raising his eyes from the path. "I didn't see any hole—no stone he could step on that I could see."

"I'm so sorry. It was my fault, I know, I shouldn't have been so strong headed. I had no idea this would happen, of course, but that doesn't excuse it."

"It doesn't signify," Jonny answered, though in his attempt to pass off her apology he was unsuccessful in keeping the emotion out of his voice, and his gaze as it met hers for a brief moment was unintentionally accusing. "It could have happened to anyone. All my fault, I assure you."

"It wasn't your fault and I feel terrible," Beth returned shortly. "It was unforgivable of me. I *knew* the animal could not keep up with Storm. But had I had sense enough to think about it, I should never have allowed you to make the effort on a mount not of my own choosing."

The dejected young man refused all her entreaties to go with him to the marquis and explain the accident, so there was nothing for her to do but return to Berkeley Square while he led the limping horse back to the stable. Once she had turned Storm over to the grooms, she retired immediately to her room and composed a missive to Lord Alspeth, taking all the blame for the injury on her own shoulders. How successful she had been she learned later that evening.

With her uncle's restrictions hanging over her head, even Beth did not dare ignore the invitation to a dinner party, to be followed by a musicale, from such a personage as the Countess Levein. When Beth and Jane arrived the drawing room was favoured with the cream of the *ton*, and after greeting her hostess, Beth was drawn into conversation with Lady Castlereagh. The famous hostess of Almack's, haughty in appearance though she might be, inclined her head graciously.

While the hostess was friendly enough, Beth was sure, by the occasional references to Lord Farling, that her uncle was the prime reason for the interest, and she was glad enough when Lady Jersey arrived and Lady Castlereagh excused herself to speak with the third Almack's hostess.

Left to herself, Beth looked around and espied Jane in conversation with Lord Alspeth. The apology she had sent him that morning did not seem to be sufficient now that she could speak with him in person, and she hurried in their direction.

As she approached, Jane smiled brightly. "You were some time in conversation with Lady Castlereagh. I think she was quite taken with you."

"For my uncle's sake only, I assure you," Beth replied and held out her hand to the marquis. "Good evening sir. I can't tell you how sorry I am about the accident this morning. I assure you it was entirely my fault, and I hope you will not lay the blame on Jonny."

Lord Alspeth made his leg and gazed down at her solemnly. "I thought you understood that there should be no galloping in the park," he said coldly.

Beth raised her chin. She had been wrong, she knew, but it was not for him to criticise her actions. "I saw no harm in it, and Storm needed to stretch his legs. We certainly endangered no one at that hour."

"I can hardly agree, since I have an injured horse, and my nephew could have come to grief."

Beth's irritation turned to anger. "My lord, I was under the impression from seeing him in the saddle that your nephew was a very competent rider. I am persuaded that had he been properly mounted, he would have had no difficulty. If he cares to ride with me again, I will provide him with an animal more likely to stand the pace."

"That will not be necessary," the marquis replied through clenched teeth. "I am perfectly capable of providing a mount for my nephew."

"Under normal circumstances, I daresay," Beth replied with no less heat. "But when he rides with *me*, it would be better if he were mounted on cattle that compares in quality. Please inform him that if he cares to join me in the morning, I will see that he is *adequately* provided for."

"I will most certainly convey your message," Lord Alspeth answered with more than a trace of ice in his voice. With a low bow he left Beth and Jane standing by the window and crossed the room to speak with a gentleman who was just entering.

Beth watched him go with smouldering eyes, but her fire was doused with shame as she saw Jane's discomfort.

"I'm sorry, Jane, but he angered me most severely. It is not his right to censure my actions."

"Most assuredly it is not, but Steven is prone to speak too forthrightly in times of stress, I fear. Still, you must admit all the severity was not on his part."

"I'm sure I don't know what you mean." Beth opened her fan and made an attempt to cool her flushed cheeks.

"Like you, he has a great affection for his animals. When you challenged his stables you challenged his pride."

=5=

THE NEXT MORNING, not knowing whether she would be riding with a groom or with Jonny, Beth was preparing for her early outing when she was told the grooms had brought Storm to the door. Hurriedly securing the pale yellow wide-brimmed hat on her titian curls, she picked up the gloves that so exactly matched both the hat and a new velvet riding habit, and descended the stairs. One final glance in the huge gilded mirror in the entrance hall told her her habit was all that it should be. She thought it a pity that so early in the morning the only viewer would be young Jonny, and then chided herself strongly. *Was she falling into the ways of the fashionable?* she asked herself.

As she stepped outside she paused, surprised. At the bottom of the steps her grooms were trying to subdue Storm, but across the pavement, sitting his horse arrogantly in the dappled shade of a tree, was Lord Alspeth. He bestrode a chestnut mount whose lines were every bit as good as Storm's, but who limited his spirited play to an occasional toss of a well-shaped head and occasional light mincing steps that rang on the pavement like bells.

"Good morning," Beth called, deliberately casual, trying to hide the elation she felt at seeing him again. "I had no idea you were disposed to favour early morning rides."

"I wasn't aware one needed to announce that particular preference on first meeting," the marquis returned with equal nonchalance. "The puppy had a prior engagement. I come as a surrogate—and to see this animal." He eyed Storm with just the faintest trace of scorn.

His expression was not lost on Beth. Had such a look been directed at her personally, she might have shrugged it off without a thought. For him to cast even the slightest aspersion on Storm was more than she could accept with equanimity. The culmination of years of careful breeding and hope by both her father and herself had been given life in that horse. If he was a little spoiled, that was not to be held against him. Seething, she kept her tongue while the groom threw her up into the saddle. She took the reins, ordered the stablemen to give the horse his head and braced for his reaction.

In justice to the well-bred animal, there was not one ounce of meanness in that beautiful body. Had Beth curbed him sufficiently to make her will clearly known, he would have settled immediately to obedience, but he had his head, he was young and strong, with a mistress light of both body and hands. He was fully aware that she enjoyed his antics as much as he. He sensed her moods quite as easily as she did his, and he knew they were in for a spirited morning. Storm was more than ready to do his part.

In the glorious enjoyment of his youthful strength and the knowledge that once she was in the saddle, he and his mistress were inseparable, he reared, balancing himself on his hind legs, starting for the park in that most spectacular manner—a rearing canter.

Beth, her hands still light on the reins, gave a full laugh. "Then feast your eyes, my lord. It seems Storm has decided to go through his paces." She could have kissed her spirited mount. Nothing could have been more beautiful to watch than his perfect balance, which he held for even longer than usual before he settled to a sidling prance, arching his neck to its fullest advantage. Even Lord Alspeth acknowledged it.

"Very pretty, but a little training in manners would benefit him." The marquis was keeping a firm hand on the rein of his own mount, who was exhibiting signs of wanting to show off what he could do.

Beth looked at the chestnut pointedly, giving her expression a hint of calculated derision. "I prefer Storm to keep his spirit," she remarked archly. "If I wanted a *palfrey*, I'd ask to borrow yours."

That remark was, she knew, unworthy and inaccurate. Barring Storm, the chestnut was the last animal that could be considered a small-boned and small-spirited mount, suitable only for a timid female rider. Her words had the desired effect, however.

The spark of anger in Lord Alspeth's eyes was equal to hers. "There is nothing lacking in Tommy," he announced, giving the horse his head. At once, as if not to be outdone by Storm, the chestnut reared to show his own balance.

Storm tossed his head, gave a whinny that signalled his acceptance of the challenge, and raised himself on his hind legs again, pacing Lord Alspeth's stallion step for step.

At that moment two young gentlemen turned the corner. Their clothing, which pronounced them the pinks of the *ton,* was a bit dishevelled by an evening that was just breaking up, even though the sun had risen over an hour before. They halted, leaned against each other for balance, and simultaneously raised their quizzing glasses, watching the two horses prancing along on their hind legs.

"Gad!" ejaculated the first. "Benny usually has bad wine, but this is the outside of enough! Dashed if I'll go there again," he said, shaking his head.

"Must have been shabby stuff," his friend agreed as he allowed his glass to fall and clutched at the wall for support. "Never had any that affected me like this—got to Alspeth too, I see."

"And his horse," the first added, turning to help his friend. "Don't remember seeing Alspeth at the party, but he must have been there—and brought his mount. Got the beast so bosky it don't know how to run."

"Don't think that's good *ton*, bringing cattle to a party," the second answered.

The first young man, apparently not quite as far gone as his friend, wrinkled his brow. "Must have been at a different party. That's a dashed pretty chit, and if there had been two horses and a female there—think I would have noticed."

His friend shook his head and looked as if he were trying to concentrate, but he gave it up as if it were too much effort.

"Don't remember, but I think you should speak to Alspeth. Want him at my card party next week and don't have room for his horse."

They nodded at each other, and, pleased at being in agreement, they linked arms and staggered off down the street.

Meanwhile, seeing that they had an audience, Lord Alspeth was brought to the realisation of their folly and reined in his chestnut.

"We're acting like idiots," he announced sharply. "This folly belongs in the nursery." He turned an irate eye on Beth, but as the corners of her mouth were recalcitrant and insisted on turning up most humourously, his irritation turned slowly to a sense of the ridiculous. What began as the start of a lecture turned into a chuckle and then a full laugh, with Beth joining in.

"Truce?" Beth asked as the explosion of mirth faded back to a chuckle again. "Can we not admit we both have non-pareils for mounts?"

Lord Alspeth leaned forward in a small bow, sweeping his curly-brimmed beaver in a courtly gesture. "I will even go so far as to admit that Storm is the first to seriously put Tommy on his mettle. If I could have seen his eyes, I believe they would have been green when Storm started his first rearing canter."

"But he had no need," Beth admitted, allowing her admiration for the big chestnut to make her compliments as gracious as the marquis's. "He is an animal anyone would be proud to own." She gave him a look from the corner of her eye. "I think you must be persuaded that when Jonny tore after me in the park, he thought he was rescuing me."

"I will so inform him," Lord Alspeth agreed. "However, I suggest that we forgo a gallop and canter from here," he said as they entered the bridle path. "I believe it will be necessary to make two trips along the course—the second one will doubtless be at a more sedate pace."

Beth caught his amused look, and she wondered what could be behind it. He continued, "I daresay there will be more riders by then and we mustn't have people thinking you are just out of the nursery. This time you may *not* lay the fault at my door. I have no expectation that the Honourable Miss Sally Rathsham has your ability on a horse. I hope you will not heap scorn on her head if she rides a palfrey."

"So we are aiding a romance," Beth smiled, remembering her conversation with Jonny two days before.

"Hardly. Jonny's far too young—his father won't allow anything serious at this stage. Then too, the chit's just out of the schoolroom."

"You must not tease him, you know," Beth warned. "The first love is always the most painful—they say."

"They say?" Lord Alspeth quizzed her.

"And it's true," Beth insisted. "I know! When I was ten there was the most handsome eleven-year-old son of the local blacksmith. I was heartbroken for—" she gave him a roguish look "—days!"

The marquis laughed. "For me it was older women. I was crushed when the dairymaid married the head groom. Nothing I could do. She was quite above my touch, of course. Several years older than my grubby twelve." He sobered. "While he is in town Jonny is my responsibility. I'm not going to throw him and the girl together, but I'm not going to give him cause to bolt for Gretna Green, either. My brother would never forgive me if he got into trouble."

They gave the horses the office and cantered to the end of the bridle trail and back. Just as they reached the edge of the park three riders appeared. Beth and the marquis drew in their mounts and waited while the trio approached.

Jonny, astride a good-looking black, introduced the Honourable Mr. Frederick Rathsham, a shy young man of no more than eighteen years who stammered out his pleasure and drew back from the group as soon as it was seemly. Miss Sally Rathsham was hardly more outgoing than her brother and blushed prettily when she was introduced.

"I hope you're not returning from your ride," Jonny said worriedly. "It's jolly to ride together in a large group, don't you think so, Miss Rathsham?"

The young woman coloured again, casting a shy look at the marquis and another at Beth. "It is much more pleasant," she said hesitantly, reaching out to pat her horse's neck.

Involuntarily, Beth traded looks with the marquis. The young lady's mount was indeed a palfrey, a quiet, elderly mare that still showed good lines but was past the age of high spirits and would never put her rider to any discomfort. No less meek was the young woman. As Lord Alspeth had said, she looked hardly old enough to be out of the schoolroom. Her riding habit was a pretty blue; the cut and style spoke of an excellent modiste. Still, it lacked dash, trimmed only with a small white cording that encircled the collar and cuffs. Like her outfit, Miss Rathsham was not in any way oncoming, an altogether mousy young lady with medium dark hair and big brown eyes that she kept lowered to the ground.

"Then it's settled," Beth spoke up brightly. "Miss Rathsham, if you will ride with me, I promise to keep this naughty animal of mine in line. However, Jonny, you must stay close in the event he takes off on one of his fits. In that case you should be by Miss Rathsham.''

"Oh, I say, I will.'' Johnny moved protectively to Miss Rathsham's side.

Their second trip along the path was most commonplace, with no incidents of untoward horseplay. Beth tried several times to draw out the shy young woman, but she was without much success. She learned the family had been in London a fortnight longer than she, but they were not, it seemed, overly active in society. Beth could readily believe it and wondered what Jonny could possibly find so attractive in a schoolroom chit who was too shy to talk.

Her viewpoint on that subject changed, however, when she fell back to speak with the marquis. When Miss Rathsham was left with only Jonny for an audience, she answered his light comments, sometimes at length, in a low, well-modulated voice. Beth listened as Lord Alspeth tried to draw out the brother, and did not appear to be succeeding until he invited Mr. Rathsham to accompany him and Jonny to an upcoming mill the following week. Gratitude made the young man verbose.

"Oh, s-sir! It d-does sound like quite the th-thing! It really d-does! Such a g-good g-go! D-Deem it an honour, s-sir! M-Much obliged for the inv-vitation! Know it w-will be the greatest thing ever!''

"Then perhaps you should discuss it with Jonny,'' Lord Alspeth said smoothly and gave Beth a look of profound relief when Mr. Rathsham hurriedly made his excuses and cantered up to join his sister and Jonny.

"I must be careful of his gratitude,'' the marquis said in a low voice. "Before he finishes his thanks, the mill could be over.''

Later that week, Beth kept her promise to Jonny, not only

by leaving her card on Curzon Street, but extending to the Rathshams an invitation to tea. Her choice of the date was even more fortunate, since Lord Farling arrived the morning of the proposed entertainment. Not aware that Beth was assisting in an affair of the heart, her uncle was disposed to look upon the small party as a sign that Beth was becoming reconciled to her stay in town.

Nothing could have been more jovial than his attitude toward Viscount Rathsham, and the circumstance of their having been at school together helped considerably. Beth considered it particularly fortunate, since their reminiscences kept them in conversation and allowed the young people to draw apart and have their own visit undeterred by their elders. The marquis had sent his regrets, being previously engaged for the afternoon, and twice Beth silently chided herself for thinking the party was dull indeed in his absence.

=6=

LORD FARLING, his visits to his friends repaid for a time, planned to remain in London to escort Beth to her court presentation. Though she disliked the season as a whole, she both looked forward to and dreaded the upcoming event that kept her uncle in town. While she made no mention of it, she was unable to share the *ton*'s blasé attitude about meeting royalty. Her major regret was the illness of the king. He, like Beth's father and later, like herself, was an experimental farmer, interested in the improvement of his land and in new and improved strains of crops and stock.

Even if he had been in the best of health, she had no thought of getting into some deep agricultural discussion at a royal reception, but the idea that she might meet someone of a shared interest was most pleasant.

Knowing her uncle put great store by their appearance at court, Jane had bullied Beth into several fittings of her gown and would not accept Myra's substitution. The dress hung carefully draped in the wardrobe of an unused guest room.

The afternoon they were to be presented, Beth sat at luncheon with Jane and Lord Farling.

"Such a busy day, my dear," Jane was saying. "To court in the afternoon, and Almack's tonight. I fear you will be quite done in."

"Don't care much for that," Lord Farling muttered as he

helped himself to a compote. "Shouldn't do too much running around in one day. Don't want to make the girl ill, you know."

Jane sighed. "I will try to be more careful, Gubby, but between you and me, we have cluttered this one day most odiously. Never mind, though, there will not be many that are so full."

"No running the girl or yourself to death, mind." Lord Farling reached over, patting Jane's hand solicitously.

Beth wondered if she had imagined the affectionate look her uncle had given her companion.

Since both Beth and Jane had their own personal maids, and wanted to retain them, it was a most unusual, albeit satisfactory arrangement in their eyes that they employ one dresser between them. However pleased the ladies might be with their plan, the three servants were not inclined to look upon it in the same light.

Myra, totally unacquainted with the fashionable hair styles and the proper arrangement of scarves and shawls, was considered too fumble-fingered to assist her mistress in being readied for her presentation. Since Jane would not be accompanying Lady Beth and Lord Farling, the dresser had entirely taken over her lady's chamber. Myra, left with nothing to do but look on, showed her jealousy, which took the form of criticism. Lady Beth quite forgot her nervousness in calming the two maids after a spate of vitriolic comments.

Thus when she joined her uncle she was so anxious to be away from the dressing room battle as to seem anxious for her presentation. Thinking she was growing to like London, he was pleased and jocular throughout most of the afternoon.

At the palace, they found themselves in line to be presented along with numerous other noble families who were bringing out their offspring that season. Once they had made their obeisance and the rigidity of the reception line had broken into smaller groups, a familiar voice close by caused Lady Beth to turn.

With a strategy she could only admire, Lord Alspeth moved, causing the other three in his group to turn, thereby including Lord Farling and his niece.

When the introductions had been settled and Lord Farling had made his leg to Lady Stilsen and her shy, lanky daughter, the marquis introduced Mr. Thorpe.

"Somehow these fellows keep cropping up every year or so, and it's one of my penalties that I have to keep bringing them around. It's a dashed bore when there are so many of them, but there it is."

"And I'm sure my uncle would say the same," Lady Beth replied.

"*I* hardly think he would say so." Mrs. Stilsen had smiled indulgently upon the remark of the marquis, but her reply to Lady Beth was chilly and more in the line of a censure. She eyed the pale cream crepe underskirt and the looped overlay of aquamarine satin worn by Lady Beth as if it were good enough only for wear in the kitchen. Since her own daughter was wearing yellow, a colour definitely not flattering to her olive complexion, the effect of her disapproval was lessened in the extreme. Not content with the derisive look, she feigned to forget the name.

"I do think, Lady—" she paused as if trying to remember something faintly disagreeable, which immediately brought up the hackles of Lord Farling.

"Lady Elizabeth Anne Haughton-Marshall!" he announced in freezing accents and a little overloud.

"What? What?" A rotund gentleman led by a footman in royal livery charged forward.

For some moments Lady Beth had been aware of him. He had wandered into the drawing room over the objections of his companion. He was not dressed for an appearance, and seemed, though adamant at being where he was, a little confused. Suddenly he came charging toward them, directly at Miss Stilsen.

"What? What? You the Haughton-Marshall girl? How's your cotton?"

Taken quite unawares, the shy young woman was in the act of drawing back behind her mother when she was summarily pulled down in a deep curtsey by the matron.

"Your majesty," Miss Stilsen whispered breathlessly.

Following the lead of Lord Farling and Lord Alspeth, Lady Beth curtsied, but pity for the frightened girl caused her to speak, drawing the attention of the blind king.

"I regret to say it did not care for my land, your majesty. The project was a dismal failure."

"A failure. I don't like to hear that!" the king said, turning toward the sound of her voice. "Takes a warmer climate I'd say."

"I think so too, your majesty," Lady Beth replied. "I tried both the American and the Egyptian strains, but with no success."

"What? What? Both strains?" The king took her arm, turning her away from the others. "Heard some things about you and your father. You doing anything interesting on that farm I want to know about?"

"Your majesty, you are complimenting me beyond my station. I am not at all in your class. I'm afraid my latest project is only chickens."

"What? Chickens, by God! Fine! Fine! If you get a good brood I'd like to have some. Send you some of my pheasants—oh, dash it, can't you tell I'm—oh very well." The last words were directed toward the attendant who was urgently trying to lead the blind king from the room. Lady Beth sadly watched him go, once more a confused old man. He held all of her attention until he was out of sight. It took no fey premonition to warn her that she would not meet the king again, but in later years she was glad to look back and hope she had lightened his last few hours of sanity by discussing with him the farming he had so loved.

"Unfortunate that he overheard me," Lord Farling said as the carriage took them back to Berkeley Square. "The odour of the provincial is not one admired in London Society."

For Lord Farling's peace of mind it was just as well that he left the house on Berkeley Square after partaking of a fine dinner with his niece and Mrs. Westcott. He retired early to bed and kept to his announced intention of beginning his homeward journey at a very early hour. He was, therefore, unaware of the stir in Almack's caused by the agricultural enthusiasms of a blind and very ill king.

A number of people who had attended the drawing room were also present at the assembly; notable among them was Mrs. Stilsen. Like many overly ambitious parents who were desirous of making good marriages for their ungainly offspring, she was constantly on the search for opportunities to put a spoke in the wheels of her daughter's rivals. To her it was a gift from heaven to be able to spread the news. Other dowagers who were fully as anxious as Mrs. Stilsen to further their offspring at the cost of anyone, were delighted to repeat the story.

When Mrs. Westcott introduced Lady Beth to Mrs. Drummond-Burrell, the haughty hostess gave a disdainful sniff, acknowledged the new arrival hurriedly, and moved away. Mrs. Westcott and Lady Beth were still pondering over her attitude when they were joined by Lord Alspeth and his nephew.

Mr. Thorpe's face was somewhat flushed and his eyes showed sparks of the most severe irritation. The marquis was clearly amused.

"Steven, you will tell me what is amiss," Mrs. Westcott

said imperiously. "We are hardly within the door, and I find three people, all with attitudes most exceptional."

"Aunt Jane, even among the *ton*, to strike up an instant friendship with the elder George Hanover is not an everyday occurrence. But to immediately begin trading barnyard fowl, well, in short, I'm afraid it will become the *on dit* of the day."

"Nothing but a lot of jealous old gossips trying to start a quiz because they have gawky chits for daughters, if you ask me," Mr. Thorpe said savagely.

"No one asked you, and you're just repeating what I said, so don't go taking the credit for it," Lord Alspeth said as he frowned at the boy. "Try giving a proper greeting to your great-aunt and Lady Beth, and put on a face they can tolerate."

As Mr. Thorpe hastily made a rather awkward leg to each of the ladies, Mrs. Westcott frowned up at her nephew.

"Should I feel I have entered in the middle of a conversation?"

"Your comment is apt, dear Aunt," the marquis replied.

"Oh, have no fear, Jane. You will, no doubt, hear it all as soon as you leave my company," Beth chuckled. "Tell me, my lord, have I been given a name? I understand that is a quite common occurrence when one becomes the subject of ridicule."

"It makes no matter!" Mr. Thorpe impatiently intruded into the conversation. "Who would listen to anything they say?"

Lady Beth laid a consoling hand on the young man's arm but continued to gaze at Lord Alspeth. "The name, sir?"

Opening his snuff box, he offered it to Mr. Thorpe before turning his attention on Beth again. "The Hen Herder, courtesy of the witty Lord Withington, who doubtless still rankles over the set-down you gave him. He now says your stories were only a cover to prevent the *ton* from recognising the truth." He gave her a sharp look. "What do you have in mind? That's a devilish expression."

Beth lowered her eyes. "Sir, you wrong me, yet at the same time, I think perhaps you credit me with more wit than I possess. I fear I must bear with the shame, not being capable of matching Lord Withington's clever tongue."

"I say! The dancing is starting!" Mr. Thorpe stepped forward to stand by Beth's side. The unseemliness of his enthusiasm overcame him and he blushed deeply. "I—uh—that is—"

The marquis gave him a pained look. "Lady Beth, will you please be so kind as to honour this young cub with a dance? Lord, will I be glad when he develops some address! Aunt Jane, would you honour *me* by taking some orgeat in my company?"

Throughout the evening Beth was cognizant of the eyes turned in her direction. There was apparently only one topic of conversation. She was not shunned, precisely. Several of the more daring young bucks sought introductions, but their conversation was desultory, since the main questions in their minds could not, with any propriety, be asked.

Altogether it was a long, uncomfortable evening, but Beth managed, with the help of Mrs. Westcott, Lord Alspeth, and Mr. Thorpe, to give the assembly the impression that she was completely oblivious to the gossip.

It was not until five o'clock the next afternoon that the polite world was aware that Beth knew of their talk, or that she might have the daring to react. To her finely drawn sense of justice, it was one thing to give society a chuckle, and quite another to have someone deliberately attempt to make another person a laughingstock.

With no one in the household did she discuss her plans. Early that morning she inspected the stables, and to one groom's surprise, he found himself with a decidedly unusual chore that would take him the greater part of the day. To Myra, her maid, she gave a list of items she wished purchased and dispatched her after extracting from the tight-lipped servant a vow of secrecy.

Lady Beth spent part of her morning writing letters to the bailiffs of her various estates, sending them through her uncle. When Myra returned, Lady Beth closeted herself within her room and refused entry even to her maid.

The afternoon had been showery, and there had been no callers, but as the hour for the promenade approached, the sky cleared and the ground seemed dry. When she met Mrs. Westcott in the drawing room, the widow exclaimed over her appearance.

"Oh, what a fetching outfit! I declare, there will not be another lady in the park to equal you. And that hat! You brought *that* from the country? Such a milliner is sorely needed in London."

As they descended the stairs to the entrance hall, Mrs. Westcott was less enthusiastic over another part of her companion's clothing. She frowned as Lady Beth began to pull on a pair of long, bright yellow gloves.

"My dear, are you sure you should wear those with *that* outfit?"

"Oh, I am quite sure. Nothing else would do." Lady Beth stopped in front of a large mirror, inspecting the finished effect. She smoothed the lines of her white batiste dress, one Mrs. Westcott had arranged to be made for her. On her auburn hair was a very large-brimmed white hat. No less than seven brilliant red ostrich feathers arched in one line, falling fore and aft of the hat in a single row. The long, bright yellow gloves reached halfway up her forearms. It was not until they were descending the steps to the street that Mrs. Westcott learned the purpose of Lady Beth's outfit. She gave a smothered screech as the groom came around the side of the house with two snow-white chickens on a leash. So white were they that their red combs and yellow legs were in brilliant contrast to their snowy feathers.

"Can't be too sure about her, my lady, but he's one high stepper, that one is," the groom said, pointing to the rooster.

"But they will walk on a lead, won't they?" Beth asked.

"Oh, they stop and peck at this and that, but they're doing fine. I'd take this ground corn if I were you, my lady. You might have to give them a bit of encouragement now and then."

"Oh, I'll take that." Mrs. Westcott rushed forward. "I have to be some part of this. Dearest, it was quite bad of you not to let me help with the preparations, but I declare, you will be a sight. Not even the odious Lord Withington can smirk after he sees you!"

Those few in society who had not heard of the Hen Herder before that afternoon's promenade were certainly informed of her before nightfall. The startling spectacle of a strikingly dressed beauty, her outfit so exactly matching the rather unlikely pets on her leash, was enough to make the gentlemen raise their quizzing glasses to stare. A series of traffic problems occurred on the carriage path. Not once did Lady Beth look around, but to those who passed her on the walk, nodding, or raising their hats, she was all normal civility. Ahead of her, a man had been going in the same direction as she, but when he noticed all attention was directed behind him, he stopped. The scene caused him to raise his glass and stand staring until Lady Beth drew abreast of him.

With an obvious curiosity that was past all bounds of good manners, he quizzed first the lady and then the chickens. His glass moved several times from the brilliant red combs of the fowl to their exact likeness on Lady Beth's hat. Then he lowered his glass and looked her straight in the eye.

"Madam, you terrify me. If you chose to wear yellow and black, would you walk a tiger?"

"Hardly, sir. That is a question you would not ask if you knew me well. I am called the Hen Herder. In an outfit of yellow and black, I would doubtless have to find a more exotic breed."

"But a more exotic vision, you would *not* make." He bowed quite low. "You must be Lady Elizabeth Haughton-Marshall, friendly farmer to kings. Your servant, George Brummell, ma'am, and I would ask a favour of you."

"A favour for the august Mr. Brummell? If it is within my power, sir, but are you sure even *your* reputation can stand mine?"

"Madam, I would risk all for a chance to take one of those leashes—no, not the rooster. You cannot imagine the joy to be derived from leading some old London hen around on a leash."

If the fates have a sense of humour, they showed it at that time, for no sooner had Mr. Brummell taken the hen's lead than a cry of "Mama, look!" caused Lady Beth to raise her eyes. The shocked face of Mrs. Stilsen as she stared at Lady Beth and the famous Beau Brummell walking the chickens was enough for her to count the day a success.

But still other victories were to come her way. Before she could turn her attention back to the path again, in a curricle coming from the other direction, she espied Lord Alspeth and Mr. Thorpe. The marquis raised his eyebrows and his hat, while his nephew waved his own curly-brimmed beaver in a circle of congratulation.

"Oh, is she the one? Well, she's giving them all the most charming set-down of the season," was suddenly heard in unmistakable Germanic accents.

George Brummell looked up from his absorption in guiding the hen. "In case you failed to recognise the voice, you have at least one hostess of Almack's on your side. Never discount the Princess Esterhazy."

"Why, sir, with your assistance and that fair lady on my side, is there anything I could not do?" Lady Beth smiled.

Mr. Brummell sniffed in disdain. "I doubt if *her* countenance could help if you shot the Prince of Wales or tried to steal the crown jewels. For either of those you would need mine." He held out his hand, offering the leash back to Lady Beth. "If you will be so good as to reclaim your pet, I feel I have had a surfeit of her hen-witted company, as charming as yours may be. I trust you will allow me to call in at Berkeley Square?"

"It would be delightful, sir."

As Mr. Brummell raised his hat and walked jauntily away, Mrs. Westcott stepped up beside Lady Beth. She sighed as she looked up at her charge.

"And after all that effort, too."

"Dearest Jane, what are you thinking?"

"Well, I certainly didn't think you did this to make the *ton* pleased with you."

Lady Beth was much struck by the idea. She thought a moment before she answered. "I'm not certain what I meant," she said slowly. "I did it out of anger over last night."

"Now that does *not* please me." Mrs. Westcott looked up at her companion with disapproval. "I will allow your right to follow your course within the limits of propriety, and even to assist you, but to act without thought in a moment of pique is a waste of a fine wit."

Since the ladies were not engaged for that evening, they were not to learn until the next day how the fateful walk had been accepted. Even though Myra had stood for fittings, and Mrs. Westcott had chosen most of Lady Beth's wardrobe, there were still a few sundry items that required the young woman's personal attention. She and Jane were out early the next morning, and on their return they were astounded to find that the silver salver in the entrance hall held no fewer than a score of cards. One of the first callers, Hughes informed his mistress with a slight touch of awe, had been Lady Jersey.

The afternoon brought Lord Alspeth and Mr. Thorpe. The young man was still jubilant over Lady Beth's now famous walk.

"It was capital, the most bang-up thing I ever saw. I say, Lady Beth, will you do it again? If you do, I wish you will let a fellow know. I'd give a groat to walk behind you and watch the faces! I say, will you let me know? It is the most famous thing I've ever seen."

"Steven, can't you quiet that cub of yours—send him back to the kennel or something?" The four people in the drawing room looked up to see George Brummell standing in the doorway.

"Hallo, George." The marquis stood lazily and offered his hand. "Matter of fact, I brought him over so I can get some advice from Lady Beth. If she can put chickens on a leash, I thought I might do the same with him."

"Might work." Mr. Brummell raised his quizzing glass and stared the young man out of countenance before bowing over the hands of Mrs. Westcott and Lady Beth.

"Good afternoon, sir," Lady Beth greeted the much touted gentleman. "Did you come to assist me with my herding?"

Mrs. Westcott settled herself again and searched in her voluminous sewing bag for her embroidery. "I am convinced I am tired of those chickens, and we must think up something else to talk about. And Steven, at the risk of making you irked with me, I will wish you to stop teasing Jonny. He is a good boy, and I will not have you forever giving him setdowns."

79

"Oh, no, Aunt! I think you misunderstand my uncle altogether," Mr. Thorpe said, coming immediately to Lord Alspeth's defence. "He has undertaken to make me a gentleman, which is more than most would do for their own brothers! Not only is he introducing me around, but he is even teaching me how he ties his neckcloth, though he has to finish mine for me—"

During this speech the marquis had glared at Mr. Thorpe, motioning him to silence, but that effect was only achieved by Mr. Brummell.

"Good God!" the beau threw his hand to his temple and let his head fall back against the sofa. "What *am* I doing in the company of Hen Herders and bear leaders? Even *my* reputation can stand only so much!"

Lady Beth looked at him archly. "I warned you, sir, that I will contaminate everyone around me."

"Then I will take myself off at once," said Mr. Brummell as he rose. "Steven, if you are not otherwise engaged, I am on my way to Jackson's. Care for a bout?"

"Oh, I say, that does sound to be the thing—" Mr. Thorpe's enthusiastic words faded as both gentlemen frowned him down. He flushed slightly and then looked back at his uncle with what Lady Beth could only describe as the expression of a chastened but hopeful puppy.

George Brummell shrugged. "You may bring him along, provided you borrow a leash from Lady Beth."

The three gentlemen took their leave, and as they clattered down the stairs, the sound of young Mr. Thorpe's excited voice drifted back into the drawing room.

=7=

TWO DAYS LATER, Lady Beth's new phaeton was delivered. Since she had been quite taken with the picture conjured up by the colour scheme Mrs. Westcott had envisioned, Lady Beth had given orders that it should be done in just that way. The addition of black harness and reins combined with the Snow Queens, Lady Beth's favourite pair, gave the promise of the carriage being more eye-catching than anything she could have done. For her first jaunt in Hyde Park, she wore the white costume again, complete with the red ostrich feathers on the hat.

Used to the narrow country tracks of the home farm, it was Lady Beth's wont to drive tandem. The horses, having received only minimal exercise since she had been in London, were fresh and restive.

Lady Beth looked closely at Mrs. Westcott, concerned that the dear lady might be a bit frightened. "Would you prefer that I took a groom just for today?" she asked.

"You would not do such a horrid thing to me," Mrs. Westcott retorted. "I declare I am quite as done up as my doltish great-nephew. I would not miss the stares we will get for the world. You just drive; I will report the expressions I see."

"You, my good chaperone, are incorrigible," Lady Beth laughed. "If you misbehave I will report you to my uncle."

"Shameful of me," Mrs. Westcott agreed. "I would hang

my head if it were not occupied directing my eyes—good *day*, Mrs. Stilsen. A lovely day for a walk.''

Before they had traversed a quarter of the way around the park they had been stopped no less than three times. Mr. Reynolds, who had been so improper as to request several times a third dance with Lady Beth in Almack's, and had four times left cards in Berkeley Square, was some minutes hanging onto the side of the carriage before the ladies could continue their drive.

A friend of Mrs. Westcott's, a Mrs. Northern, hailed them and spoke a few words. They were hardly moving when the estimable Ladies Jersey and Sefton drew abreast of them.

Silence, as Lady Jersey was called, had numerous flattering comments to make about the white rig. By the time they were ready to move again, the Snow Queens were prancing in place, tossing their heads impatiently.

Despite their strength and high spirits, they were superbly trained and had very tender mouths, leaving Lady Beth in no doubt that she was in complete control. Nevertheless, as they rounded a bend in the path and came upon the halted phaeton of the exact same style, Lady Beth's team gave every evidence of being ready to bolt.

Like her own, Lord Alspeth's rig had undergone a change, though it was less noticeable. He had replaced the brown upholstery with a more fashionable buff shade, but what caught the ladies' attention were the startled faces of two occupants and their companion on foot as they looked up. Lord Alspeth and Mr. Thorpe sat in the carriage. Mr. Brummell, with one foot placed negligently on the step, seemed to have been in conversation with them. The three were wearing expressions of that particular horror when one sees a disaster in the making and is helpless to prevent it. Unable to resist showing off her considerable skill, Lady Beth whipped her rig over, coming to a halt with less than two inches to spare between the outer wheels of the two carriages. The Snow Queens continued to prance in their harnesses as if there had been no slackening of speed, but the phaeton was perfectly still.

"I really don't believe it!" Mr. Brummell ascended to the top step of Lord Alspeth's rig to look at the prancing pair.

"I pray you will forgive their manners, sir, but they are anxious for a run." Lady Beth said calmly. "Just youthful exuberance, you know."

"Right ones!" Mr. Thorpe whirled around, putting his knee on the seat. "Bang up to the knocker!"

Lord Alspeth looked at the white horses carefully before turning back to greet Lady Beth. "They are beauties, right enough." He gave her a smile of approval. "They certainly didn't come from Tattersalls."

"No, sir. They did not," Lady Beth replied, feeling unaccountably pleased with his approval. "I herd other things besides chickens, you know. These are home-grown."

"Did you raise them?" Mr. Thorpe's eyes widened. "I'd give a groat to see them raced!"

"Young sir, you do seem determined to give away your groats," Lady Beth laughed. "But in that instance they wouldn't be wasted. I've yet to set them against anything that really challenged them." She looked back at the beautiful chestnuts driven by Lord Alspeth, wondering if they were as fast as they appeared to be. Mr. Brummell mistook her meaning.

"Steven, you've just been challenged," he said.

Lord Alspeth's laugh was more derisive than civil. "My lady, these are champions, nearly retired for want of a challenge. There is nothing in London to touch them."

Lady Beth saw the glitter of pride in his eyes, but she felt just as strongly about the Snow Queens. "Nothing until my ladies arrived," she retorted.

"Very well, madam, find yourself a driver and I will pace my pair against yours. Shall we say tomorrow at ten at Farnham Track?"

Not trusting herself to speak, Lady Beth nodded and

wheeled off at a fast clip, leaving the gentlemen to stare after her.

As they drove around the park, Mrs. Westcott was silent for some time. Then she gave a gusty sigh.

"Do I offend you, dear Jane?"

"Offend me? No, dearest, of course not, though I must say you overset my nephew a bit. His horses, too, are home-grown as you say, and his pride in them is the outside of any-thing reasonable. But it was odious of you to agree to race *to-morrow*. I am convinced that I do not have a hat for such an undertaking. I suppose the blue will have to do, but still I cannot think it will be dashing enough."

"Jane, you certainly will not be riding in the race!"

"Then do I misunderstand you so completely? You will actually allow someone else to drive these beautiful horses?"

"Certainly not! No other hands but mine have ever held the reins on them, nor will they ever do so. The Snow Queens have very delicate mouths."

"It's just as I expected," Mrs. Westcott nodded em-phatically. "The blue hat will have to do."

The ball that night was a crush, the first such crowd that Lady Beth had experienced. From the moment of her arrival she had been deluged with partners, and Mr. Thorpe was hard pressed to get even one dance. By the time he made his way to her side for the quadrille, she felt overcome with the heat and the crowd.

"I say, I don't like your look," he said, frowning at her.

"Now, Jonny, that's no way to court a lady." Lady Beth gave him a playful tap on the wrist with her fan, but for once the young man was not embarrassed by his tongue.

"Oh, you're done up to the first water, and you know it, but you're dashed pale."

"To tell you the truth, sir, I think I'm becoming a vapourous female. I abhor the thought, but I don't feel well."

84

"If you mean just tonight, it don't signify." Mr. Thorpe put his hand to his snowy cravat, which had wilted on the edges. "I ain't too keen on this crush, and that's to say nothing about how Aunt Jane is taking it. Fact is, Steven said something about taking her home."

Lady Beth looked anxiously toward where she had last seen Mrs. Westcott. "If she is unwell, we should certainly leave. Would you mind missing this dance?"

"Not at all," he said graciously, though his attempt to take her arm was done somewhat clumsily. "I'd as soon leave off dancing completely, but if I have to, I'd rather it was with you."

"My, how graciously said, sir. Your uncle would be proud of you."

Mr. Thorpe blushed. "Well, I mean to make him proud of me, ma'am. He don't like me to say it, but there's not many that would take the trouble he has for me. He don't like this kind of thing above half, you know. He only came to London to get me set."

They had some difficulty making their way through the considerable throng, but presently they espied Lord Alspeth taking a cup from the hand of Mrs. Westcott. The widow looked as pale as Lady Beth felt herself to be.

"I'm afraid my aunt should return home. The puppy will escort you later, if that meets with your approval—" Lord Alspeth's voice trailed away as he looked hard at the younger woman.

"Well, it don't," Jonny replied. "It's too hot and too crowded for Lady Beth, and me, too. I'd as leave see them home and you can stay."

"Lord, I'm not staying," the marquis said, surveying the crowd. "In any case, I want to see Aunt Jane home."

Fortunately, all that was needed to revive the health and spirits of the four was the cool air of the evening. They were so refreshed by the time they reached Berkeley Square that Lady Beth called for a cold supper to be prepared and they settled down to a quiet game of whist. She and Mr. Thorpe were unmercifully beaten by Mrs. Westcott and Lord Alspeth, but the losers took their defeat with good heart.

The stiff attitude evidenced by Lord Alspeth in the park had vanished. His conversation was heavily laced with his droll wit, abetted by Mr. Thorpe's efforts to emulate him. Twice Lady Beth raised her eyes from her cards to find his eye on her with such an enigmatic expression that the second time she was so confused she made a foolish discard. Only the hilarity of Mr. Thorpe and an equally outrageous mistake of his own relieved her embarrassment.

Had they remained at the ball they might have been better prepared for what they found the next day when they came in sight of the smooth track on the Farnham Property, a beaten path that had seen many a race between members of the *ton*.

As Lady Beth drove around the bend she was astonished to see what appeared to be at least a hundred vehicles placed along the sides of the course. Lord Alspeth's phaeton was just drawing even with the starting line. After a momentary pause, Lady Beth wheeled up beside him, looking around with some consternation.

"My lord, what is this? I had no idea half the city would turn out to see us race. How did so many hear of it so quickly?"

Lord Alspeth shrugged. "I would suppose someone in the park overheard us." He wrapped the reins around the knob on the seat handle and jumped down. Two quick steps and he was at the side of Lady Beth's rig, assisting his aunt to the ground.

"Bring up your driver," he said to Lady Beth. "We'll check the rigs over and then we'll see who has the fastest pair."

"My lord, I am my driver. No other hand has ever touched this pair."

Lord Alspeth looked thunderstruck. "Surely, you have no

idea of racing in public?" he asked. "Ma'am, I cannot race you! It would cast a slur on my name to so disgrace yours!"

Lady Beth bit her lip to hold back hasty words. She strongly resented the veiled accusation that she would be so lacking in decency, yet she could appreciate that it might look so. She spoke quietly.

"I fear it was my ignorance and not my lack of taste that has brought us to this pass. When I spoke of racing, I thought there would only be the four of us, or five if Mr. Brummell had cared to come. In my part of the country it is not thought exceptional for ladies to race one another, or even compete with gentlemen on the privacy of their own estates."

Mrs. Westcott put her hand on her nephew's arm. "Steven, dear, neither of us had any idea there would be an audience."

"I see," the marquis replied slowly. "My apologies to you, Lady Beth, if I seemed short. I should have known. Much of the blame is mine, I think. Nevertheless, your coming here alone will cause some talk."

"My dearest nephew, you must not talk fustian," Mrs. Westcott said sharply. "When we learned our driver was indisposed, how should we not ride out and appraise you of it? We did not think it at all the thing to send a message by a footman when we must cry off after offering the challenge."

The marquis, still frowning, patted his aunt's shoulder. "Trust you, Aunt Jane, to see the answer when the rest of us are still looking at the problem. Perhaps it will serve."

While the four at the starting line had been talking, the crowd was growing restless. Close by were a number of dandified young men who appeared still somewhat under the influence of their late evening. Their demands for the race to start had gone unnoticed by the occupants of the two phaetons, but they intended that they should be heard. With their arms about each other's shoulders for support, they counted off and then in one voice shouted, "GO!"

In their impatience they had been drawing nearer to the starting line, so when they shouted they were close to Lord Alspeth's pair. The chestnuts were off like a shot. Lady Beth, who had let her reins go slack in her hand, was caught unprepared when her own horses leapt after the others. Recovering her balance, she was gathering the ribbons to pull up when she saw Mr. Thorpe trying to reach across the phaeton, making a desperate effort to free his reins from where they had been tied down on the seat handle.

Just at that moment the left front wheel of Lord Alspeth's rig struck a pothole, and the jolt threw Mr. Thorpe back against the seat. Dropping her hands, Lady Beth sprung her horses, hoping to draw alongside and assist young Jonathan.

From long experience on the Farnham track, the marquis's team knew exactly what they were about. No guidance was needed to tell them they were to round the pole at the other end of the course and return to the starting point, and at all costs they were to do it before their rivals. No less knowledgeable were the Snow Queens that ran at their side, since they had often raced on the home farm. To Lady Beth's team, the only difference was that they were accustomed to drawing a vehicle far weightier than the featherlight rig they were pulling at the moment. Their desire for victory was as great as their opponents'.

In the black phaeton Jonny was trying to ease his way across the seat so he could reach the reins still tied to the knob of the handle. The light rig, occasionally striking potholes, literally flew across the ground after the straining horses. The swaying of the well-sprung vehicle caused him to abandon his effort and hold on to keep from being flung into the air.

In the white phaeton, Lady Beth urged her beasts on, her eyes anxiously turned to the young man in the runaway rig. She had no intention of racing and was only trying to keep pace with Mr. Thorpe in the hope that she could somehow assist him. Their fast approach to the post, therefore, had no meaning for her.

For the horses, the whitewashed pole was the halfway point in their goal. Both teams, free of the errors of human guidance, knew just how close they could come to the post and to each other without snarling the wheels of their rigs. Seldom given the opportunity to take a turn at maximum speeds, they were not so knowledgeable about the balance of their vehicles. Thorpe, unable as yet to reach his ribbons, could not slow his team. Lady Beth had forgotten she was on a track and made no effort to slow hers. When the horses reached the post, they went around at full speed, throwing their weight into the turn for balance. Behind them the two phaetons careened sharply to the opposite direction, causing the occupants to hurl themselves against the upturned sides.

Lady Beth could not resist the cry that came up into her throat, but had it been the shriek of a banshee, it would not have been heard over the roar of the crowd gathered at the starting line. Never had they witnessed a race in which a female was driving, nor had any who traveled out to the Farnham track that day ever seen such breakneck driving.

Still the show was not over. Tearing back to the finish line, the pair of chestnuts, straining side by side, and the Snow Queens were taking their heads. All four were of a long lineage of racing stock. As if they had planned their own strategy without the aid of humans, neither would allow the other a lead. Several times Lady Beth tried to pull her rig closer to Lord Alspeth's, but the chestnuts would not allow it, nor were the Snow Queens as amenable to her demands as usual.

They were nearing the finish line when she saw with relief that Mr. Thorpe had finally untangled the ribbons and was gathering them in his hands.

The roar was deafening as they shot across the finish line together and fully three furlongs farther before they were able to slow and turn the horses back to where the others were waiting.

Totally shaken, Lady Beth automatically brought her pair to a halt on the road beside those of Lord Alspeth. Frozen in her position, she could not at first even turn her head. Mrs. Westcott was handed up into the phaeton by the marquis, whose face was white. His voice was hoarse with fury.

"Madam, I trust you have had enough excitement for the day and will be able to conduct my aunt home in safety?"

Still unable to control her breathing, and very much upset by the impromptu race, Lady Beth nodded, not understanding his meaning.

"Then please put your cattle on the road this instant!" His voice was a hiss.

There was nothing left within Lady Beth with which to argue, nor to question his anger. Raising the ribbons, she set the Snow Queens at a gentle trot, moving back toward London. It was not until she had turned the phaeton and pair over to her groom and had taken a seat in the drawing room that the numbness of the frightening experience wore off. Tears flowed down her cheeks as she sat, too exhausted to wipe them away.

"I thought Jonny would never be able to get the ribbons," she said.

Mrs. Westcott had remained silent all the way home. She had removed her hat and stood for some moments looking into the fireplace. Now she turned back to her charge.

"What ribbons, dearest? How could he have driven the race if he didn't have the ribbons?"

Lady Beth looked up blankly. "But Jane, there was no race!" She told Mrs. Westcott what had not been seen from the sidelines. " . . . and thankful that neither of us suffered an injury—Jane, why do you look so strange?"

Indeed, Mrs. Westcott sat weakly in a chair, her bottom jaw slack. Then she rose and began to pace.

"My dear, you tell me it wasn't a race. If you say so I believe you. While I, along with all society, know you to be overly fond of a lark, I am persuaded you draw the line at making a spectacle of yourself. But I must tell you, dearest, that from the sidelines it *did* look to be the most breakneck of sporting events. I heard more than one gentleman say he had never seen one to equal it. I am much afraid that it will be most thoroughly discussed and not forgotten for many a day."

"Oh," Lady Beth put her hands to her face and sobbed. "I am utterly ruined."

"Now, that I cannot see," Mrs. Westcott replied in a matter-of-fact tone. "Granted it is not the thing, but every lady in society can drive a curricle or some type of conveyance. To drive a phaeton and do it faster than most is not such a sin that it should ruin you. It is not offensive after all. I am convinced we can weather it. Society forgets, you know."

"Society can hang, for all I care." Lady Beth jumped to her feet, pacing about the room while her tears still streamed unregarded. "It is my uncle who concerns me. If he thinks I did this only to be allowed to go home, I may never get back my farms."

Just as painful to Beth was the memory of the anger on the face of Lord Alspeth, though she couldn't admit this to his aunt. The lack of colour, she thought, would have been due to his shock and disgust. Without a word she ran from the drawing room, but as desperate as her flight might have been, the bitter memory kept pace with her.

With her energetic nature, it was very unusual for Lady Beth to take a rest during the day, but a short time after she returned from the Farnham track she retired to her room. Exhausted as she was, sleep took her quickly, and it was well into the afternoon before she awoke. She washed her face, changed her clothes, and tidied her hair, forbearing to call her maid. Quitting her chamber, she went quietly to the drawing room, opening the door and entering before she realised Mrs. Westcott was not alone. Staring into the fireplace, his back squarely to the room, was Mr. Thorpe. His voice was hoarse with emotion.

"Dash it, Aunt Jane, I have no intention of repeating it. Uncle Steven's opinion of me is not fit for a lady's ears, but it was said, and if he can believe that of me—well, it is insupportable, that's what it is!"

"Jonny, dear, he was more frightened than angry. He was terrified out of his senses when those carriages went around the post. Dearest, none of us thought either of you could come out of that alive! Pay no attention to what he said. He had to stand there helpless and watch—*that* is insupportable for a man like him."

"No, Aunt Jane, you don't understand. You knew when I got here what happened. You listened—he wouldn't! I don't know how I thought he could care—well, I know he's dashed well glad to be rid of me if he feels that way! I'll not bother him again!"

Suddenly he wheeled and headed for the door, apparently not even seeing Lady Beth until he had almost collided with her. As he came close, she saw the blinding tears in his eyes.

"Jonny." She put out her hand, but he drew away.

"All I can say to you, my lady, is that I will see you get your deserts!" With that he was through the door and clattering down the stairs.

In the drawing room Mrs. Westcott and Lady Beth exchanged astounded looks; his last statement had left them speechless.

=8=

"I CAN'T GO—I just can't face them," Beth insisted for the third time as Jane demanded she return to her room and don her promenade outfit.

"But you must, dearest," Jane was adamant. "There is nothing for stopping talk like stepping forth and meeting it. Remember, you can only talk behind a person's back if that person is turned away from you. The best way to mend this problem is to act as if nothing untoward has happened."

"But the promenade will be nearly over," Beth argued, looking at the ormolu clock on the mantlepiece. Above all things she desired to return to her room, not to dress and stroll in Hyde Park, but to disappear from the world until the wounds of the day had healed, relinquishing her pain.

"So much the better if we are late," Jane returned, unperturbed. "The number of people we'll have to see will be limited, but I assure you, word will be all over town by tonight that you were not quelled. It will go a long way toward mending matters."

Shaking her head, unable to believe anything or anyone would be able to undo the impression she had made on the polite world that morning, Beth, nevertheless, retired to her room. There she donned a soft rust walking dress, heavily bordered at the neck, sleeves and hem with white French embroidery. In the large gilded mirror she eyed the rust kid walking boots she had thought herself fortunate to find because of their exact match to the dress. She wished she didn't have to display them for the first time in such unhappy circumstances. With a sigh she allowed Myra to secure her shawl in place with a pearl brooch and tied the ribbons of her chipstraw bonnet.

Myra's chatter was no comfort at all. It had been beyond hope, of course, to think the gossip that must be raging all over the city had missed the ears of her own servants, and the maid was doing what she could to make her mistress feel better by expounding on her desire to return to Carthalin Hall. Beth answered in monosyllables, not daring to voice her own opinions, too grateful for the support of the ageing servant to allow the woman to know her every word was piercing her mistress's heart like a knife. It was a relief to escape Myra's soothing efforts, even though it was to face the society of the promenade.

As Beth had forewarned, it was late when they arrived on the paths where the *ton* took their afternoon strolls. Jane set both the pace and the mood of their walk, suddenly becoming animated in her conversation. As they passed several people they knew, she gave a sketchy bow, but appeared so deep in conversation they had no time for lengthy greeting. Due to the hour, most of the more fashionable had left the park, and, as Jane had prophesied, the few they met were too astounded to suddenly find Lady Beth on the path to remember to give her the cut direct, even if they were so inclined.

"Oh, no," Beth murmured, breaking in on Jane's lively tale of a visit to France. "It's Mr. Brummell himself."

"Good," Jane nodded, her eyes dancing. "Nothing could be better."

"You don't understand," Beth hissed. "If he turns his back on us, I may as well start packing for my return, and my uncle will never forgive me."

The famous Beau was at that moment just turning from a carriage where he had been in deep discussion with a gentleman and a lady not of Beth's acquaintance. Neither of the three had seen the approach of the two women. As Mr. Brummell tipped his hat and stepped back from the vehicle, he turned in their direction, his curly-brimmed beaver still raised as he caught sight of Beth and Jane.

Beth knew she was being cowardly, but she busied herself with searching in her reticule for her handkerchief while she pretended to listen to Jane's discourse on the beds in French inns. Out of the corner of her eye she saw her companion give only the sketchiest of nods to the unchallenged leader of London society and continue her lecture as if he had been one of the trees in the park.

Beth was unable to resist a peek from beneath the brim of her bonnet and thought nothing could have been more ludicrous than the look on Mr. Brummell's face. The gentleman who, with one lift of an eyebrow, could make or break any aspirant's hopes in the *ton* hardly expected to be ignored by the one person in London who needed his help most. The surprise with which he received this lack of respect had held him on the path beyond the time he could gracefully turn away. He raised his hat higher and gave a small bow.

As Beth and Jane were only two paces from him, the small plump widow gazed at him directly with no sign of welcome. He looked from Jane to Beth and back again, his face a study of indecision.

"I warned you, sir," Beth said as they paused in their walk. "I seem to besmirch everything I touch. Do take yourself away before you too are ostracised."

"I?" He raised his chin and gave her an astonished stare.

"I'm afraid what she says is true," Jane said sadly. "We certainly would not wish you to become a victim of our follies, so, if you will forgive us, sir, we will leave you."

"I assure, you, ma'am, I am in no danger."

"I cannot accept that, sir," said Jane, shaking her head.

"You have been so good as to rescue us from one scrape, but we will not be so unthinking as to risk your credit again." So saying, Jane gave him another nod and moved on, with Beth following in her wake.

"Madam!" George Brummell's voice was imperative, causing both ladies to halt immediately. His quick strides brought him even with them before either could object. Beth looked up to see his handsome features grimly set.

"I am not a flat, and I will not be gulled."

Jane's eyes flew wide. "Gulled, sir? Do I misunderstand you? In admitting we are in bad odour, and not wanting to contaminate your unsullied reputation, I am gulling you? How am I doing so?"

"You're throwing out a challenge. You're daring me to show I have the power to overset the damage of that race—" his features softened as he looked at Beth "—and I've never seen ribbons better handled."

"But I really didn't—" Beth wanted to explain, but the shock of the day was wearing off and her innate pride would not allow her to grovel.

"You didn't what?" Mr. Brummell grinned. "You didn't win the race the way you expected to, or you didn't expect the reception you encountered at the track? It was an idiot thing to do, but if you must act outrageously, it's best to do it with a flair, and that's certainly what you did."

"But I still think you can't undo it," Jane said doggedly. Her eyes were snapping with humour as she looked up at the well-dressed gentleman.

He threw back his head and laughed. "Dear lady. All that was wanting in that race was for you to have been with Lady Beth, and unless I misread you completely, that is your major regret. I accept your challenge. We will call it an exercise in my influence, if you like. I've been too long with nothing to truly interest me. One grows dull when one is bored."

"It's too much," Beth protested feebly, and only for the

sake of good manners. Her mind at the moment was on the dust her uncle would raise and the risk of losing control of her farms permanently, as well as on the look that had been in Lord Alspeth's face.

Brummel threw out an arrogant hand. "Possibly it will hold my interest for a few days, and give a new topic of discussion around the clubs. All I ask of you is to hold your head up. No apologies, no excuses. If you're going to wear the colours of a nonpareil, then wear them with style. I cannot abide shabbiness. I will call for you at eight and you will accompany me to the opera this evening. The Marchioness of Linsford had the bad manners to fall ill."

With a bow he turned on his heel and marched off, leaving the two ladies staring after him.

Beth, disbelieving her good fortune, stood with her mouth open, but Jane caught her hand and led her away. They strolled on for a few minutes in silence, Jane looking smug and Beth casting glances at her companion from time to time.

"I knew the world would be in danger if you ever turned to crime," Beth stated. "How did you dare? Or did you dare? Did you know you would receive that reaction?"

"I wasn't sure," Jane answered, "but I didn't think we had much to lose, and you, my dear, set it up beautifully, not only today, but on our first meeting here in the park. Do you remember when you asked him if his reputation could stand yours? I merely acted upon the stage you contrived."

Even under the auspices of the fashion leader, Beth was nervous as she entered the prominent box in the opera house. All over the theatre, quizzing glasses were turned in her direction. All her willpower was centered on trying to appear at ease, nodding and replying to George Brummell's comments as he spoke of this one and that one, bowing to some, smiling at others, pointedly ignoring still others.

"The Countess of Colwaite," he murmured as he bowed to a buxom woman weighted down with rubies. "If she invites you to her country place, either have a previous engagement or take influenza—infinitely preferable, I assure you."

"Most wise," said Jane, sitting immediately behind Beth. "The only thing more discomfitting than the meals on her table is the terrible heat that pervades the entire house. I declare she could hatch eggs by laying them on the drawing room carpet."

"Surely not quite so hot," Beth laughed.

"But exactly," Brummell answered with nonchalance. "There is one thing worse, however, and you would be extremely conscious of it. The earl's hunters are the most jarring bonesetters in the country, and you'd be called on to admire them."

"Then I am persuaded I will have a previous engagement or influenza," Beth replied, grateful for their attempt to make her evening more pleasant. "I cannot abide admiring bad breeding."

Further conversation was prevented by the lowering of the lights and the start of the performance. The music was good, the singers excellent, and Beth was lost in the entertainment. When the first intermission brought back an awareness of where she was, most of her discomfort had vanished.

As usual there was a stir among the boxes, with a great deal of visiting back and forth, and it was not to be thought peculiar that George Brummell's box was beseiged by those who desired to be seen in his company.

One visitor who could not be said to be under the influence of the fashion arbitrator was the Honourable Mr. Coster. He shook hands with his host and begged to escort Beth and Jane on a search for refreshments. They had only just left the box when Jane slowed, and Beth saw Lord Alspeth approaching. He too paused, apparently not quite sure he should approach. Beth saw a tightening of his lips as he looked at her and her heart seemed to fall to her toes.

When it was clear that the marquis was not going to come up to them, Jane was torn between staying with her charge and going to her nephew. Beth felt the least she could do was to free Jane of that one concern.

"Dear, shall we bring a glass of ratafia?" she asked her companion. "If you would care to stroll with the marquis, we will be glad to procure refreshment for you."

After Jane squeezed her hand in gratitude and hurried over to join her nephew, Beth continued on with Mr. Coster. All her joy in the evening's entertainment had been shattered by the look the marquis had given her. The anger, the contempt she thought she saw in his expression at the race track was absent, but the friendliness, the affection of the earlier days was gone. Nor was the next person she encountered to do anything to alleviate her depression. As they rounded a corner of the passage, they came upon Mr. Frederick Rathsham, who was leaning against the wall in a brown study.

"Good evening, Freddie," Beth said with forced cheerfulness, hoping he would not cut her, but deciding she must risk it.

"Oh, g-good evening," he stammered as he made a hasty and awkward leg. "G-Glad to see you. Want you to know that was a d-dashed fine bit of driving this morning. Wouldn't have m-missed it for the world."

"Thank you," Beth said quietly. "But not everyone thinks so, I'm afraid."

The Honourable Mr. Rathsham scowled. "Lot of f-fustian nonsense. Told m'father so at d-dinner—" He stopped in considerable confusion, his face reddening.

"Oh, dear," Beth sighed. "I had hoped he would turn a deaf ear to the talk. I so liked your sister, and hoped we might be friends."

The young man's scowl deepened. "Stupid, th-that's

what it is, and so upsetting to S-Sally too. M'father's told her she's n-not to be in the company of Jonny anymore.'' He straightened, lifting his chin. ''N-Not that I'm going to be dictated to. Jonny's a great g-go, and I'll tell anyone!''

Wisely, though a bit belatedly for Beth's peace of mind, Mr. Coster made his excuses to Mr. Rathsham and led her away. She tried to make suitable responses to her companion's light conversation, but neither his chatter nor the wine could raise her despondent spirits.

Haughty and arrogant were two words often used in referring to George Brummell, but no one had yet to call him either insensitive or stupid. Whether he recognised in Beth the desire to remain inside her shell of misery, or he had a natural disinclination to spend much time in the principal company of a young lady not disposed to light-hearted conversation, his earlier mention of a small supper at Grillon's took on larger proportions. The guests included those whose names had been on every invitation list, and in addition were among those whom Jane had indicated were people not to be affronted. Seen in their company, Beth knew her worries about being ostracised were relegated to the past.

Supper was a sumptuous affair, with a sideboard loaded with creams and jellies. Beth ate two lobster patties and sat with a group being regaled by the wealthy banker's daughter who had married the Earl of Jersey and become a leader of society. With Silence, as she was called, holding the floor, Beth joined in the occasional bursts of laughter and let her thoughts wander as they would.

She found it difficult to get her mind off Jonny's pain, knowing he must be severely hurt by Viscount Rathsham's disapproval of the race. Had she allowed her mind to run in that direction, she would have recognised the parallel between her concern for the boy's feelings and her own hurt at the reaction of the marquis.

The evening, the sparkling glasses, the candlelight reflected in the mirrors of the private supper room, the laughter of the company all seemed unreal. She smiled, responded out of training and good manners, but she was relieved in the small hours of the morning when the party was over. Finally, in the privacy of her room, she could droop her shoulders and succumb to the misery she had been holding back since that morning.

Though the approval of society was not, and had never been, her aim, she was indeed grateful to George Brummell for his assistance. When he had taken Jane and her to the opera, Beth was under the impression that that favour would be the extent of his help and she would probably not see him again soon. She was, therefore, astonished when an hour after noon of the following day, a message was brought to the small salon; Mr. Brummell had called and was waiting to be shown into the drawing room.

"Good morning, sir." She crossed the room to meet him. She was glad she had chosen a green and white figured muslin with dark green ruching at the neck and sleeves that morning. As her guest bowed over her hand, the elegance for which he was noted was apparent in the perfect fit of his dark blue coat and the delicate hue of his pantaloons. To receive him in anything less than the first style of fashion would have to be an affront to his person. She was certain his hessians could have been used as a lady's mirror.

As he rose from his bow he looked solemn. "My dear, I came to thank you for a pleasant evening, but I must tell you, all our efforts were wasted."

Beth, totally missing the twinkle of amusement in his eye, was considerably lowered in spirits by his announcement. She offered him a seat and chose a Chippendale chair facing him.

"I'm sorry," she said. "But you must know that I appreciate your efforts in my behalf. If you have suffered any hardship—"

"I?" He raised his chin haughtily as he interrupted,

bringing up his quizzing glass to inspect her as if she had been a specimen on display. "I assure you, my dear, I have not suffered. You have totally mistaken my meaning. If I have any regrets over the evening, it is that I bestirred myself to accomplish something, and I no sooner leave my house this morning than I learn my efforts were unnecessary. Your true benefactor, and I cringe to admit it when I was convinced it was I, was young Thorpe, Alspeth's bumbling nephew."

"Jonny?" By now Beth was thoroughly confused. Fashionable Mr. Brummel might be, but she thought he was somewhat oblique in his comments. "Jonny is my benefactor? I'm afraid I don't understand."

For the first time since his arrival the Beau smiled. "I can hardly fault you for that. I found it inconceivable that this awkward cub could best me in anything, but I must give the boy his due, I suppose. While we were doing the pretty at the opera, he was making the rounds of the sporting clubs, and, it seems, announcing himself as the most honoured gentleman of the *ton*. He has taken the title as his due, being the only man in London that has had the lovely Lady Elizabeth Haughton-Marshall race to save him from a runaway team."

"Oh, poor Jonny," Beth gasped. "He'll make himself a laughingstock! He mustn't do that for me."

"Not at all." Brummell crossed one elegantly shod leg over the other and took a pinch of snuff. "In his blundering way he's making you out to be a heroine and still coming out in good odour, I think. He says Steven's team ran the course, and you kept up in an effort to assist him."

Beth nodded. "But from Jane's description of what everyone saw, who would believe it? I went to the track expecting to race, so who would believe it was an accident? I had no idea it was a public place, you know."

"My God, how disappointing! I really think that's what

bothers me the most. The most interesting race in some years was run by accident.''

"Sir, if you think I would take any prank that far, I have given you a false and shabby opinion of myself. Not that I could fault you for it, however.''

Brummel raised his glass again and surveyed Beth through it. "Are you telling me that the other pranks were accidents too? That is carrying belief a little far, my dear.''

"No, I don't pretend they were,'' Beth sighed. "But I've had my fill of them. I've learned my lesson. There is too much risk and nothing to be gained.''

"Ah-h, what an altogether disappointing morning,'' the Beau sighed. "Now we are to be bereft of the most interesting series of *on dits* to enliven a season in years. I think I will retire to White's and try to overcome my despondency. I confess I thought, when you learned young Thorpe had effectively averted a scandal, you might set to work weaving some new scheme, and that I would be the first to know of it. I almost missed the race, you know.''

His twitching lips made Beth smile. She said, "Well, this I *must* promise you. If I decide on another, I will be sure to send you an invitation, but I have every intention of putting my career as a jokester aside.''

"Ah, well,'' he sighed as he rose. "Then it's White's for me. Perhaps I can salvage something. I *can* say I knew it was a rescue attempt, and who would doubt me, since while all the *ton* was talking, I escorted you to the opera.'' He straightened his shoulders, raised his chin a little higher, and looked down at Beth. "Perhaps I'll gain a reputation for being omniscient. It could add to my esteem if you don't give me away.''

Beth dimpled. "I will do what I can, but do you really think it will serve? I mean there is also an *on dit* about a dice game at White's earlier this week—'' Beth bit her tongue, wondering if in mentioning Mr. Brummell's gambling losses she had committed a breach of manners.

His brows lowered, but he pursed his lips thoughtfully. "I quite agree—omniscience and gambling losses don't go together, do they? Well, I'll think of something else."

At that moment Jane entered the room. She was out of breath; just having risen from a nap, she had rushed her toilet. Her preparations for coming into the drawing room were noticeably hurried and her lace cap was slightly askew. With only a nod to Beth, she went straight to Mr. Brummell, heaping on her elegant visitor her gratitude for the previous evening.

"Madam," he interrupted with hauteur, "I hardly find it seemly for you to bore me with your thanks for something I have not done. I will leave you to be further enlightened by your lovely companion." He bowed over Jane's hand, made his leg to Beth, and took his leave.

Jane fluffed her skirts in frustration and looked more than ever like a hen with her cap skewed over one eye. Watching her tardy chaperone, Beth could no longer restrain her laughter. As Jane turned her head back and forth from the door where the Beau had disappeared to Beth and repeated the action several times, Beth gave way to a severe case of the giggles. Whether Jane was being comical out of her confusion or whether she continued it for Beth's amusement, Beth didn't care. It was good to feel free of the burden. She and Jonny were out of trouble.

Not long after, a footman came in with a tray bearing a decanter of port and one of ratafia, as well as glasses. While the servant took his time about arranging the items on the tray, once he had set it on the small table by the confidante, Jane bustled about giving him hard looks that showered her impatience on his livery-shod back.

Beth understood her impatience. Not until the footman

left the room could they discuss Mr. Brummell's news, which he had only intimated to Jane. When the door was closing behind him she dashed across to Beth, only to have Hughes enter again, bringing in the marquis's card.

"I do declare!" Jane murmured when Beth read out the name. "Two gentlemen catching me with my cap on crooked." She rushed to the mirror to straighten the lace confection.

"I'll retire to my room," Beth said, rising and hastily drinking down her glass of ratafia. "Your nephew will doubtless be more comfortable if I'm not here."

"Doubtless," Jane agreed, still looking in the mirror as she fussed with her cap. "But if you do, I have not the slightest doubt he will come looking for you. It is you he's come to see. I was going to prepare you for his visit, but things are sadly askew with me this morning."

Beth took her seat, folding her hands in her lap, trying to still her quaking heart. She pushed Jonny to the forefront of her mind, trying to concentrate on the injury to the marquis and what it had done to the boy's pride and heart. She dared not think of her own. It seemed that she could feel every muscle in her body drawing up into tight little knots, as if even her toes felt they must be on guard to keep her innermost feelings from showing. When the marquis entered the room she was so stiff she wondered if she would be able to do a creditable job of rising.

She kept her eyes lowered as he greeted his aunt, but courtesy demanded that she meet his gaze as he bowed over her hand and she was shocked at what she saw. For her the time since the race had been an ordeal, but it was readily apparent in his face that he too had suffered. There were small lines around his eyes that had not been noticeable before, and his cheeks looked to be sunken, yet tight from the strain that showed along the sides of his jaw.

"My lady, I am here to extend to you my apologies," he

said in a tired voice. "I would have spoken to you last night, but the opera is too public when two people are both upset. I am aware my behaviour at the track was unforgivable, however, I hope you can find it possible to be more merciful than I was disposed to be." The words were stiff, whether from the strain or because he felt it necessary to make an apology he could not feel, Beth wasn't sure, but she chose to believe the latter.

"Your feelings toward me are of no moment, sir," she replied gravely, choosing her words carefully to hide her new pain. "It is the hurt you have brought to your nephew that concerns me. Mr. Thorpe was entirely blameless."

She saw the pain in his eyes. "I am fully aware of that, even if my knowledge is sadly belated. I will do what I can to make it up to Jonny. Perhaps he will understand how I felt when I saw the phaetons careening—but that is between him and me."

Jane came forward and laid a hand on Lord Alspeth's arm. "I know he'll understand, Steven. Anyone would who saw the race and cared for the drivers." She gave Beth a meaningful glance. "Only someone seeing the danger and not being able to help in the smallest way could understand the fear and frustration we went through."

"But you forget, neither Jonny nor I were standing on the sidelines," Beth said. "I can try to sympathise with your point of view, but to have someone you care for believe you are capable of actions that bring dishonour on both yourself and others is a matter hard to understand by any but those who have suffered it." She was grieved to bring more pain to the marquis, but for Jonny's sake the full import of his suffering could not be minimised.

She also told the marquis what the stammering Mr. Rathsham had said about his father's disapproval and how Jonny would be prevented from seeing Miss Rathsham again.

Her sense of fairness demanded that she take some of the blame on her own shoulders.

"I fully realise that the original blame is entirely mine, because of my pride in the Snow Queens," she admitted. "I will see Viscount Rathsham and give him the full explanation. I am convinced that by now he must have heard the story that is circulating. Even if he doesn't approve of me, he must see that Jonny is without guilt."

"It's good of you to offer," Lord Alspeth said, "but again, that is something I must do. It was my loss of temper that threw the fat into the fire. We might still have brought it off without a scandal and wounded feelings if I had kept my own temper." He clenched his jaw and stared into the small fire on the grate.

"Both you and my nephew were blameless—I know that now. Your pride in your horses didn't cause this to happen without the same feeling in me, you know. The full responsibility lies on my shoulders, and I'm the only one to carry it."

So saying, he gave both the ladies a bow and left them. Jane watched him go, tears in her eyes. When the door closed behind him she dashed away the moisture that had trailed down her cheeks and tried to smile. Her voice was a falsetto of cheerfulness.

"I do declare! The men leave this house most hurriedly. What a reputation they must be giving us."

"Jane, I am so sorry. I hated to say those things, but he must be made aware of the pain he's given Jonny."

"I know you meant it for the best, dear, but he doesn't need any more incentive to find the boy and make it up to him. Years ago Steven's temper caused an estrangement with his brother Fred, and he carried a burden of that guilt for years. To do the same thing with Fred's youngest son—well, as much as Steven cares for the boy, the issue of peace in the family is once again at stake."

Jane went to the table and picked up the untouched glass of port she had poured for the marquis. She swallowed the contents in one draught, shaking her head as she lowered the glass.

"Well, someone should be able to forget about all this, and after that, I think it will be me." She dropped into a chair and stared into the fire, head down, her shoulders drooping in her depression.

Beth took the seat on the other side of the grate and acknowledged her own sad feelings. Lord Alspeth had said all the proper words, but the feelings of friendship, the camaraderie they had been building, had not been there. She had lost a friend. Friend? In her heart she knew her feelings went deeper than friendship.

═9═

AS MR. GEORGE Brummell had prophesied, Beth was a heroine. Because of the humour in his account, Jonny's story of the tied reins and the runaway team circulated everywhere. Even the ladies who raised their eyebrows when they had seen her driving the high-perch phaeton in the park had complimented Beth on her courage and quick thinking.

The invitations that had poured in from the first had come to a sudden halt for two days, but they picked up again immediately and increased in number. Not only did the buff envelopes arrive at every mail, and the cluster of cards on the silver salver in the entrance hall continue to grow, but Beth was often accosted at entertainments by would-be hostesses who were so anxious for her presence that they reinforced their invitations with spoken requests.

At a fête on Curzon Street, Jane surveyed Beth in wonder as Lady Sefton sailed away, pleased after being assured by Beth that Lady Elizabeth Haughton-Marshall had every intention of attending her ball. Jane fanned herself rapidly.

"I declare, I have not the slightest idea where we are to find the time for all this running about. I know I have muddled some dates. Tomorrow we must check our calendars."

"Not tomorrow," Beth contradicted her. "If we are to do half what we have promised, it's back to the modiste. I've run myself threadbare." Suddenly Beth laughed. "What happened to all our ideas of avoiding society? I'm still trying to discover what went wrong."

As if in answer, Lady Jersey approached, a tall gentleman in tow. She smiled at Beth and Jane and laid a hand on the man's elegantly clothed arm, introducing him to Beth. Jane greeted Baron Erthwin, with whom she obviously had been acquainted for some time. He remarked that he had seen Lord Alspeth at Watier's, and the conversation appeared to be taking a direction leading to all their various friends and relations when Lady Jersey interrupted.

"We will leave you to a comfortable cose later in the evening, but at the moment I am far more interested in having Baron Erthwin meet someone who was actually raised in Tibet."

Beth met the twinkling eyes of the famous hostess without a blink. By now she knew what was expected of her. With a flip of the wrist she opened her fan, moving it idly back and forth.

"Lady Jersey, I cannot think what wit has been quizzing you so. I would advise you to give him a proper set-down the next time you see him. I didn't think there was anyone who didn't know that my home is in the extreme northern part of Ireland, though I must say, I am surprised that so few of the English realise how far north my homeland does extend."

The baron's eyes narrowed thoughtfully and he rubbed one well-cared-for hand across his chin. "What's that? I mean, we have maps, you know."

"English maps," Beth replied scornfully and watched Lady Jersey hide her face behind her fan. "I'm sorry to say so, sir, because it's not good manners to cast disparagement on one's guest country, but your view of the world is vastly inaccurate. I find most people think of Ireland as a country with a mild climate and much like yours, but the truth is, we extend into the arctic. I'm from the north, where the snow seldom melts."

There was a pause in the conversation while Beth waited for the baron to ask a question, but he was apparently still working on the inaccuracy of English maps. While he frowned and stared off into space, darting glances were exchanged between Lady Jersey, Beth, and Jane. Lady Jersey, impatient for the joke, picked up his cue.

"But, my dear, how can a living be made off land in such a cold climate?"

"Oh, we do very well there," Beth answered. "We raise artichokes, you know."

"Artichokes?" The baron's attention was caught again. "Impossible! Climate's not right at all."

"It's quite good for them," Beth countered with serenity. "Cold just improves their coats. Didn't you know artichoke fur is becoming all the rage?"

"Gammon!" The baron's vociferous ejaculation turned heads all over the room, and there were several laughs as the other guests realised that yet another member had joined the ranks of those caught by Beth's jokes. The baron looked around, saw the knowing smiles, and turned back to Lady Jersey, shaking his finger at her.

"One day you'll get your come-uppance, Sally, girl." He eyed Beth with a wide smile. "So you're the chit that tells the taradiddles. Should have known you'd be the first one Sally brought me to see." He leaned closer, lowered his voice and winked at Beth. "Did that gudgeon, Arsvin, swallow that one?"

"I'm persuaded he did not," Jane replied. "This one is entirely new."

"Do give Lady Beth credit," Lady Jersey laughed. "She is not known for telling the same story twice. That's what makes them interesting."

The baron rocked on his heels as he frowned at Beth. "I warn you, girl, you'll have to get another one ready for when I call. I'll do that as soon as I get your direction."

Beth opened her mouth to give him her address, but he held up a restraining hand. "No, don't tell me. I'd look dashed silly leaving a card at the establishment of a modiste or some such. Couldn't trust a word you said, but I want to hear them anyway." He laughed at what he considered his own joke and strolled away with Lady Jersey.

Jane tapped Beth playfully on the wrist. "My dear, a fine wit, the ability to make people laugh without making them the targets of barbed thrusts, is an amazing talent. It certainly is appreciated."

"Is it?" Beth asked quietly. "I feel as if I'm a freak in a travelling show. I cannot like it when I am introduced and expected to perform like a trained bear."

"No one thinks of it like that," Jane chided her companion. "Everyone likes to laugh, and they like the person who can give them pleasure. You are too hard on yourself."

"And I made the place I now occupy, that's what you are really saying."

The rest of Beth's compliments were forestalled by the sight of Mr. Freddy Rathsham threading his way between the groups on the floor as they waited for the music to begin again. Beth had purposely kept vacancies on her dance program so she would have a place for him if he chanced to arrive at the party. In the short time of his acquaintance with Jonny, the two young gentlemen had become fast friends. Beth was desperately hoping he might have word of Mr. Thorpe.

Two days before, Jane had returned from a shopping trip, clearly agitated. No sooner were she and Beth alone than her tears broke free. With the release of her emotion had come the news that Jonny had taken himself away, no one knew where, and the marquis was diligently searching for him. The only certainty was that the boy had not returned to his father's home near Towbridge. Only part of Jane's tears were for the young man. The strain, she said, had aged the marquis dreadfully. He was in a torment of guilt.

Beth, watching Mr. Rathsham approach, was hopeful, but as he bowed over her hand and asked for permission to lead her out on the floor, he showed no sign of good news.

"Lady B-Beth," he stammered as he chose a set that was just beginning to form. "I n-need your help, I think, but you must not t-tell anyone."

"You've found Jonny?" Beth whispered.

"First, p-promise not to tell Lord Alspeth." He glanced furtively around the room as if expecting the carvings on the pilasters to be listening.

"But he's so worried—he's searching everywhere." Beth could not get Steven's distraught appearance from her mind.

"N-No." Mr. Rathsham was adamant. "It m-must be you and no one else. I gave my word." His weak jaw was set in an unexpectedly strong line. "C-Can't let any of his family know. Gave my w-word, you see. D-Didn't mention you."

"I promise. Mr. Rathsham, can you take me to see him? We must talk him into either returning to his uncle's house or going home. He shouldn't be in London on his own—he could get into trouble."

"Is in trouble, that's m-my guess."

"Then I must see him, Freddy."

Mr. Rathsam's expression showed his consternation. "Not the th-thing at all. C-Can't take you there. No place for a l-lady."

"If you don't take me, then I will tell Lord Alspeth," Beth threatened. "He'll see your father, and there will be a terrible dust raised."

Freddy paled. "N-No. Don't d-do that! M'father will nab the rust for sure. W-Won't like me even knowing about that b-bunch Jonny's seeing. Group of ivory turners if you ask me." The young man's eyes met hers and she saw behind the fear a genuine concern. "Jonny n-needs talking to. Won't listen to me. I'm d-dashed worried about him, Lady Beth."

"Meet me in Green Park at ten tomorrow morning," Beth said with decision. "We'll go to him, and I want to reach him before he's left his rooms for the day."

"D-Don't like it, taking you there. D-Don't think Jonny will like it either."

"Never mind, just be in the park at ten," Beth replied.

The music started, and since the dance was a lively country step there was no opportunity for further discussion. Beth was much relieved that Mr. Rathsham was given no chance to voice the objections she saw building in his expression. For the rest of the evening she contrived to keep as much distance between them as possible. She was aided by Viscount Rathsham, who had stood glowering while she and Freddy had been dancing.

For the rest of the evening, a particular excitement filled Beth, and when she was asked about her history, which occasioned another three times during the evening, she responded with such a wit that twice the dance floor was nearly bereft of dancers as people gathered to listen and laugh at her ridiculous tales.

Even her weariness after an energetic evening would not allow Beth to sleep. Her innate practicality stringently insisted she was being foolish, but visions of bringing Jonny and the marquis together and soothing the damaged feelings led to other more blissful thoughts of Lord Alspeth's gratitude. It could even bring about the return of his friendship—his love? She pounded her pillow, giving force to that practical side of her character, warning herself that nothing but heartbreak could be expected from building hopes without foundation. Still, when she began to drift into sleep, the images came back again.

The next morning, in an effort to escape Jane without

risking questions that would be difficult to answer, Beth hurriedly made up a list of errands, dividing it in two parts. She breakfasted early, and, leaving one list for Jane, announced she was off to Bond Street on foot. Myra, who could be counted upon to face drawing and quartering rather than give away Beth's secrets, accompanied her. The displeasure of the maid, however, was something with which Beth knew she would have to contend.

"Sneaking around like a hoyden," Myra said as she stumped along at her employer's side.

Beth would not allow herself to be daunted. "Will you tell me how a person can sneak, when it's obvious that we are on the street, in the full view of both the sun and the town?"

"Oh, la, it's the wit that's the rage of London, is it?" Myra evidenced a disapproving frown that was a privilege reserved for servants that had seen their employers in leading strings. "Well, you needn't use it on me, young lady. You're off for some assignation, and I don't like it. There will be something to pay if Lord Farling learns of it."

"And he will as soon as you tell him," Beth replied calmly.

"I've a mind to. It's not for the likes of me, knowing my duty and all, to let you do something shocking."

Beth ignored the threat. No matter what her actions, she was sure she could depend on Myra's silence. Still, she felt a sense of guilt, knowing the faithful maid was suffering an acute discomfort believing Beth might possibly be meeting a suitor so ineligible that she must make plans for a clandestine affair. In a low voice she quickly sketched the events that she was sure were well known to Myra and told about her arrangement with Mr. Rathsham.

". . . I gave my word, Myra. Someone has to reach that young man, and who else is there, if he refuses to see his family? Now you must keep the secret with me."

"Not that I'll be liking it one bit," Myra grumbled, "but

I'll be there to see no trouble touches you in that foul place.'' Myra straightened her already rigid shoulders, twitched at her bonnet to make sure it was secure, and held Beth's furled parasol in front of her like a weapon. Marching along at Beth's side with a demeanour more akin to that of a soldier charging into battle than a demure maid of some years, she nearly collided with a young pink of the *ton* who was at that moment sauntering down the steps of an imposing residence. He automatically raised his hat, but one look at the grim-faced maid with the parasol clutched like a rapier and he shied back like a startled rabbit.

Beth nodded politely, suppressing a smile as she heard his hurried footsteps fading away in the opposite direction.

"Dear Myra," she chided. "Endeavour not to look so formidable. You'll wear out your frown before there is occasion for it."

"And you just let my frown be, young lady," Myra retorted, not at all chastised. "I'm getting in a bit of practice, not being one to leave things go until the last minute, you understand."

Mr. Rathsham, when they came upon him on the carriage path that wound through Green Park, was visibly relieved to see Myra, but his expression showed that the alleviation of one worry had brought on another. Beth saw his anxiety, and would have explained, but Myra, with her customary directness, was the first to speak.

In scathing tones, she told him what she thought of a young gentleman who would involve a lady in such a scheme, and allowed him to know that she was there to protect her mistress, if he was not capable of doing so. The maid's words had such a profound effect on the young man that he appeared ready to bolt among the trees, leaving the two females and the hired hack behind, when Myra suddenly decided she had harangued him enough and ushered him and Beth into the carriage as if they had been small children.

Less than an hour later, after a series of turns and twists that would have done credit to the greatest enemy spy, Beth was helped from the carriage. She was overheated from the closed vehicle and irritated with the attempt at stealth that had given the driver, by his look, the opinion that she was engaged in some clandestine romantic affair.

As Beth looked about, she was glad to see that the neighbourhood was by far less squalid than the stammering young gentleman had led her to believe. She was led into a sagging house, through a narrow entrance hall, up two flights of steps that boasted threadbare carpeting and smelled musty from indifferent cleaning. The visitors stepped into a small parlour crowded with shabby but serviceable furnishings.

On a round table in the middle of the room was a masculine conglomerate of snuff tins, a box of cigars, a curly-brimmed beaver hat topped by a pair of tan driving gloves. To one side, a pile of sporting papers—one was *The Racing Calendar*—was flanked by another stack of single-sheet advertisements. The topmost was seen to advise all those interested to attend an upcoming mill to be held near Wells.

On the opposite side of the table, the remains of a morning repast was being hastily cleared away by a shamefaced servant who clearly looked upon the debris of a meal as something unfit for a lady's eyes.

"J-Jonny will be in straightaway," Mr. Rathsham, who had first entered to prepare Mr. Thorpe for the visit of the ladies, explained. "Not quite dressed to receive v-visitors, don't you know. B-Be here shortly."

He escorted Beth to the end of a sofa and awkwardly indicated that Myra join her mistress. With a sniff clearly meant to imply she needed no stripling to tell her her duty, Myra sat, tight-lipped, stiff-backed, holding the parasol in front of her.

Beth was about to tell her companions that she found their protection both confining and unneccessary when the door opened and a short, square man entered. Though she had only a moderate memory for faces, she was sure he was no guest of the *ton* hostesses. While she might forget a face, his style of dress rendered him most memorable. He was a caricature of all the extreme affectations of the Bond Street beaux. From his pomaded locks, tortured into an overdone *de Elegante*, the too-high collar points, the grotesque padded shoulders of his coat, the pinched waist, and abundance of fobs and jewelry, he had outdone every pink of the *ton* in exaggerating all the worst of the current fashion.

By the distaste clear on Mr. Rathsham's face, Beth knew her initial reaction of disapproval was shared by him.

"My dear Lady Elizabeth," the man said as he crossed the room. He brushed against Mr. Rathsham, pushing him aside without apology or even acknowledgement. Seizing Beth's hand, he bowed over it, then grasped it in both of his, expressing his sensibility of the honour she was paying him by visiting his humble abode. Beth thought both his words and his dress were at variance with his small, sharp eyes. He looked and sounded like a bobbing block, but the glint from beneath his lashes was wary and insolent.

"Sh-She ain't honouring you!" Mr. Rathsham's attitude was belligerent. "This is J-Jonny's place. He p-puts out the blunt for it. She's here to s-see him and nobody else."

Beth cast a grateful look at the young man and tugged at her hand, which the dandy seemed disposed to keep between his two damp palms. He straightened, looked for the first time toward Mr. Rathsham, giving him the cue that he expected an introduction. Freddy, with lips as tightly compressed as those of Myra, remained silent. The look that this bad imitation of a fashionable gentleman gave the boy was interpreted by Beth as being dangerous, but he turned a bland smile on her.

"Well, my dear—Lady Beth, is it?" The would-be dandy widened a smile that went no further than his tightly-stretched lips. "Since the proverbial cat has got the tongue of our tongue-tied friend—" he paused to laugh at his own joke while Mr. Rathsham blushed angrily—"I'll introduce myself. I'm Major Cable, lately of his majesty's forces. Ready and willing to come to your assistance any time, my dear." He reached up a hand as if to pat Beth on the cheek.

She drew back, disliking his leering as much as the presumption of his trying to touch her.

"Thank you." She allowed her voice to ring with frost. "I assure you we have no desire to detain you. Jonny will be here at any moment, I trust."

"Oh, no inconvenience at all, glad to be of service," he replied cheerfully. He took a step toward the sofa, for the first time acknowledging Myra's presence, and ordering her, with a flick of his eyes, to give up her place to him. He swept his coattails aside and made as if to sit between her and Beth.

Never moving her eyes from some obscure point on the far wall, nor relaxing the tension in her tightly-folded lips, the maid suddenly flipped the parasol she was carrying, dropping the handle to the floor, planting the pointed ivory end of the sunshade deliberately where the major would feel the point of her objection. For an interminable moment he was balanced in a half squat, ready to come down on the sharp point. Beth held her breath, both glad and sorry that he caught himself in time to prevent an embarrassing incident.

He rose, glowering down at Myra, and was further angered by the naked amusement in Mr. Rathsham's face. What the outcome would have been, Beth was left to wonder, because at that moment the Honourable Mr. Jonathan Thorpe entered the room.

Beth was struck by how thin he was, and by his drawn look. He appeared years older than the innocent boy who had clattered gaily down the stairs at Berkeley Square. The slightly askew collar points and the crumpled neckcloth showed he had hastily donned his attire, but in comparison with Major Cable, he was truly elegant. For a fleeting moment Beth felt pity for the man, who had no conception of quality as Jonny represented it.

Only when Jonny's gaze fell on Beth and his eyes lit with delight, did she realise how sad the boy had been. She stood and held out her hands, smiling as he made his leg.

"I've missed you," she said quietly. "Somehow, tea isn't the same without you."

The naked happiness in Jonny's face faded and in its place came an assumed nonchalance that sat precariously on a countenance too inexperienced to wear it successfully.

"So sorry. Meant to get over, really did, but you know how it is. Too many things to do. Good intentions—" he waved one hand airily.

"We've been on the run, haven't we boy?" Major Cable stepped to his side and dropped an arm about his shoulders. "There's just too many friends, too many invitations, no time for anything, it seems, but we can drop in to see Lady Beth anytime—have to make time for that."

"D-Don't remember her inviting *you*," Mr. Rathsham spoke up militantly. "Don't r-remember her saying anything about coming here to see you either. She came to s-see Jonny. D-Don't see why you can't leave them alone to t-talk in peace."

Major Cable assumed a hurt look and addressed young Thorpe. "If you feel you would be more comfortable, now that your fashionable friends have come to see you—" Beth felt her anger grow.

"No, no," Jonny objected with embarrassment, and threw a dark look at Mr. Rathsham. "The major is my guest too."

"Of course," Beth answered sweetly, determined not to let the smooth-tongued man get the best of them. "I cannot believe, however, he would have any interest in our gossip, and I do have so much I want to trade with you. Pull up a chair and let's have a comfortable cose while we can. We seem to have been travelling in different circles.'' She wondered how she was going to bring Lord Alspeth into the conversation, but it was the major who solved that problem for her.

"Jonny has been developing a new set of friends,'' he said, smiling complacently. "Friends who don't turn on him over a silly misunderstanding.''

"No misunderstanding is silly when it has caused so much pain." Beth looked at Jonny as she spoke. "Right now your uncle is searching for you everywhere, and the hurt he gave you is nothing to what he has been suffering. He knows he was wrong and desperately wants to apologise and make it up to you.''

While Jonny bit his lip and stared down at his feet, the major answered for him.

"Those are fine words, and no doubt his lordship has played a part for you, miss, but the boy knows the right of it. True friends never doubt a person, no matter what.'' His eyes challenged her.

A retort was on Beth's lips, but Jonny spoke first.

"The major is right. If my uncle had really cared a whit for me he would have taken the time to listen.'' His jaw hardened, but Beth thought she saw moisture under his lashes before he hurriedly turned away to stare into the fireplace.

"True friends are the ones who stand by you no matter what, and I've learned that lately,'' he muttered.

She saw his shoulders straighten and, as he turned, the profile of a jutting chin.

"That's not quite true, Jonny,'' Beth argued. "Those who really love you—those who care deeply for you—can never be counted upon for even-tempered feelings. They fear too much, they hurt too much. I am now persuaded that Lord Alspeth's rage was not because he doubted you. It was simply the vent for his fear that you and I were in grave danger. Just talk with him. A gentleman like you is always large-minded enough to accept an apology."

She had reached out, taking his hand as she pleaded with him, seeing the indecision on his eyes. Major Cable had been watching both her and Jonny while she spoke, but when he caught her glance, his expression was mocking.

"Ah, the pretty romantic notions of lovely ladies. They have such soft hearts, they never understand what transpires when a man's honour has been slighted. Never mind, boy, she means well."

"Honour has n-nothing to do with it," Mr. Rathsham said shortly. "N-Not in families. Always squabbles in f-families. You l-listen to this Captain Sharp, Jonny, and you're g-going to be in trouble. He k-knows Lord Alspeth would show him the d-door quick enough, and he'd h-have to find another pigeon to pl-pluck."

Major Cable glared at Mr. Rathsham. "Your tender age is all that protects you, boy. But don't push that too far." To Jonny his tone was wounded. "I'm sorry, but I can't stay here and be insulted any longer. If you choose to return to your uncle and his suspicions, I'll leave."

"I-I don't." Jonny choked out the words. His eyes snapped as he turned on Mr. Rathsham. "I'll not have my friends insulted in my own establishment. Now you must excuse us, Lady Beth. We have an appointment—already late." Suddenly he didn't seem to be able to meet her eyes.

Beth rose, holding out her hand to Jonny. His effort to take it was momentarily forestalled by Major Cable's attempt to do so, but Beth, having had enough of the man's interference, pointedly withdrew it and offered it to Jonny again.

As the boy rose from his bow, he searched her face. "You gave your word to Freddy that you would not give my direction to my uncle."

"I always keep my word," Beth answered primly. "I doubt it would bring him any solace to see the company you are keeping."

She swept out of the room, regretting her parting remark before she reached the street. She was at the moment the only link between Jonny and the marquis. If she alienated him over the odious little major, there would be no one to bring the boy to his senses.

=10=

"WHAT IS A Captain Sharp?" Beth asked as the hack pulled away after they disembarked in Green Park.

"An ivory t-turner," Freddy replied darkly. "Leads flats like J-Jonny into gaming hells—gets a percentage from the house when they lose."

"But doesn't he know that?" Beth was horrified that she had left the young man in such company. "Didn't you tell him?"

"W-Wouldn't listen. You s-saw how he was. No great harm d-done. He'll end up under the h-hatches—his father will bail him out and p-pull him home. T-Teach him a lesson. St-Stubborn gudgeon! W-Won't listen to sense."

Added to her worries over Jonny, Beth's concern when she returned home empty-handed was the speculative look she saw in Jane's eyes. It was Myra who saved Beth explanations by starting a harangue about trudging all over town when Beth was in no mood for shopping. By the silence that followed the maid's complaints, Beth knew Jane's doubts had not been put to rest, but there was, mercifully, no more conversation on the subject.

The season was by this time in full swing, and hardly a day followed that did not require a choice of various entertainments. Breakfasts, outings of several types, including picnics, left little time for receiving or paying visits, and when she and Jane were at home they were seldom alone. Almost every night Beth came home late from a rout or a ball, footsore and tired. She longed for July, when she could return to Carthalin Hall.

On a rare morning when the social activities had also taken their toll on Jane, she entered the breakfast room in Beth's wake, her cap askew, her usually good spirits left behind with her dancing slippers.

"I'll be glad to go home," Beth remarked as the footman opened the door to the breakfast room.

"And *I* think I deserve an invitation to go with you," Jane replied crossly. "How I long for some peace and quiet."

"What's this?" Lord Farling, who had been sitting by the table with a cup of coffee and a copy of the *Gazette*, looked up. He stood, his welcoming smile turning to a frown. "You are to help my niece enjoy her season, not encourage her in wanting to leave it."

The accusing look he gave Jane raised her hackles, and she answered with asperity. "Don't be a ninnyhammer, Gubby! Thirty years on the town should have taught you something. I'm persuaded it's either feast or famine, always. If Beth does as you ask, and she's popular, she is run to death and so am I. What good does it do for you to say 'don't ruin your health,' when there's Lady Jersey's breakfast, Lady Oglesby's picnic, and Lady Castlereagh's ball all in one day? Who do we ignore?" With that startling outburst, Jane burst into tears and fled the room.

Lord Farling stood with his mouth ajar until Jane was out of sight. Then with an oath he threw his paper aside and started around the table as if in pursuit. Beth, still in the doorway where she had stopped in surprise, came sufficiently to herself to catch his arm, restraining him.

"You must not follow her, Uncle. No lady wants to be seen with her eyes red and swollen. Very ungallant of you."

He tugged weakly at Beth's hold on his arm, making a show of wanting to follow Jane, but seemed glad enough to return to his chair. He cast several glances at the door and then turned wide blue eyes on Beth.

"Well, I really must say—I do think—what in heaven's name has come over Jane? Never knew the chit to have so much spirit."

"You never—" It was Beth's turn to stare, but she let his observation go. "We were surprised to see you here. Have you just come from Dorset? How are things at home? How is Lady Anne?"

"Haven't been to Dorset," Lord Farling answered automatically as he turned his gaze to the door again. "Sarah writes there is too much rain. Seems she's adopted your chickens. Never saw such women for messing around where they shouldn't be." He gave Beth a hard look. "How is it these fool women in town have to cram everything in one day? Thought they could manage better than that. Castlereagh, Sally, and Louise not talking to each other?"

"Of course they are," Beth answered, pouring a cup of coffee. "It isn't the three of them precisely, but there do seem to be more invitations than time, and who do you ignore?"

"Humph." Lord Farling settled back in his chair, his lips pursed, his brow furrowed as he thought. To Beth, he looked like a puzzled cherub.

"Should have known better than to leave two womenfolk on their own. Never seem to manage—now, don't get your feathers ruffled, girl, I meant in town. Think maybe I should take the two of you to Brighton for a few days. Not much doing there since the regent is here. Sea air and rest. That's what you need."

"No." Beth was firm. "I have engagements in town, and I don't want to break them." Her excuse was weak in reasoning but she had no thought of leaving London until she had contrived to get Jonny and Lord Alspeth to make peace again.

"Females!" Lord Farling ejaculated. "First you say you don't want to come to London, and now you say you won't leave! There's no making any sense of any of you!" He pushed away his plate and started from the room, but a thought stopped him. "And you'll do no more racing, girl!"

"How did you find out about that?" Beth's question was a retort. "Have you been staying in town without our knowledge?"

"No!" Lord Farling roared. "I came in late last night and stayed at the club. Why is it I can never enter there without being regaled with some escapade of yours?"

"You demanded I come to London," Beth replied sharply. "I've kept all my promises, I've just kept them in my own way."

Lord Farling made no reply, but his footsteps as he marched down the hall and the slamming of the bookroom door was a clear indication of his mood. His hasty exit had left the door to the breakfast room open. Beth, in no better humour than her uncle, and fully as fatigued as Jane, was taking her irritation out on a serving of strawberries, a circumstance that would have gained her a set-down from the capable cook if she had been present, when the clearing of a throat caused her to look up and find Hughes standing at her elbow.

"There is a Miss Rathsham to see you, my lady," he announced in accents of strongest disapproval. "The young Person is in your private sitting room—in Tears."

"I really need more tears this morning," Beth murmured as she rose. Not until she was on her way to her apartments did she wonder why Hughes would put a guest into the more private family quarter of the house, but the answer to that question met her at the door of her sitting room. She faced a tight-lipped Myra standing guard in the hall.

"I'll not be having Hughes or a footman bothering the child," the maid said, a dangerous sparkle in her eye. "The poor thing is half out of her wits with worry and coming here alone and all."

Beth nodded wordlessly as the old servant marched off down the hall. The butler's sense of propriety had been offended at the arrival of an unescorted young lady, and somehow, Myra had been, if not in the front hall, at least close enough to overhear Miss Rathsham's arrival and take the girl in hand. Beth sighed, and, hoping a contretemps between her servants would not be added to her problems, entered the sitting room.

Miss Rathsham was indeed upset. Her bonnet had been laid aside, and she was giving full rein to the tears that were flowing copiously into a lace handkerchief. She was such a pathetic-looking little figure with her drooping shoulders and her mousy brown curls falling forward around her face that Beth quickly closed the door and went to her side.

"Miss Rathsham—what's happened?"

The young woman jumped like a startled deer. Over the lace of her handkerchief she threw Beth a frightened look and tried to gulp back her sobs.

"I'm s-so sorry," she gasped. "You must think me the most silly person." Her shoulder shook as she fought to control her tears.

"Not at all. Sometimes a good cry helps," Beth replied. Not being prone to the vapours herself, she wasn't sure of the veracity of that statement, but it was one she had often heard and read in novels. It seemed, however, that offering the young lady the opportunity for a good cry was having the opposite effect. With a valiant effort, Miss Rathsham ceased her sobs, blew her nose, and sniffed several times.

"I apologise," she said stiffly, suiting her posture to her tone of voice. "But I have been so worried. Have you any idea what it's like to love someone who is under a cloud? First my father said I was not to see Jonny—but I still had Freddy. He helped me keep my courage up. Now he, too, says I must not think of Jonny anymore. Oh, it's so terrible! Everyone has turned against him.'' She buried her face in her handkerchief and started sobbing again.

"Not everyone," Beth replied. "I don't believe Freddy has either. He was very worried about Mr. Thorpe, but they had words when we tried to talk Jonny into—" Beth wanted to bite her tongue, but it was too late to get back the words.

Miss Rathsham's head flew up, the tears forgotten on her pale cheeks. Beth wondered what had happened to the shy young lady she had met in the park. It occurred to her that the girl might have been affecting her shyness to appear interesting, but she chided herself for the thought. Remembering the painful blushes, she decided the desperation of the girl's feelings had caused her to lay aside thoughts of herself.

"You've seen Jonny? How is he? Is he unhappy? Has he fallen in love with someone else?"

"Of course he hasn't," Beth answered crossly, thinking it was a very immature young woman indeed who sat beside her on the confidante. It had not occurred to her until that moment that as intense as her feelings were, Miss Rathsham might be far more worried about the loss of her first romance than the problems Jonny faced. She thought about giving the girl a set-down over what seemed to be mere selfishness.

"Can you take me to him?" Miss Rathsham asked breathlessly. Her face, still splotched with tears, smoothed into an angelic smile as she focused on some point in mid-air. She was clearly envisioning herself as a ministering angel to the poor but still adoring young man.

Well, why not? Beth thought. As hen-witted as the girl might be, she could still be the very one to bring Jonny to his senses and get him away from Major Cable. Her pleas, which might seem childish to Beth, could very well prevail with a very young man where older, wiser counsel would go unregarded.

"It would be unthinkable to take you to his quarters," Beth said, but hastily suggested an alternative as Miss Rathsham's face fell. "But I'll send him a message, asking him to meet us in Green Park."

"Green Park?" Miss Rathsham looked doubtful. "Do people of consequence go there? Would it not be better to meet in Hyde Park?"

"Green Park," Beth repeated firmly. "From my one visit there it seemed to be frequented principally by denizens of the playrooms and their nurses. Think of what your parents would say if you were recognised, which you very likely could be in Hyde Park. You did slip away this morning, did you not?"

Miss Rathsham nodded. "But I'd face the wrath of cannibals for a chance to see Jonny." Her words sounded brave enough, but the glance she threw over her shoulder caused Beth to wonder if she expected a band of savages to attack from the dressing room.

"We'll send him a note and have him meet us," Beth said as she rose to go to the small lacquered desk. She was halfway across the room when Myra entered through the door from the boudoir.

"I think it had best be me you send on that errand, my lady," she said grimly. "Trumbril can drive me, but no one else can be counted on not to hand your message to that vermin of young Mr. Thorpe's."

Beth smiled. She wrote her note and twisted it into a screw. Trumbril was the largest of her grooms, a big, burly fellow who lived in worshipful dread of the lady's maid. Wild horses would never drag from him what the acerbic Myra told him to keep to himself. Since the irrepressible woman heartily disliked Major Cable, she would be looking forward to having words with him, and by the time she reached Mr. Thorpe's residence, her carefully worked out store of cutting remarks would be sufficient to slice down larger game than she would find there.

With an hour to spare before they would be obliged to begin their stroll to the park, Beth ordered tea and showed Miss Rathsham the dressing room where she could repair the damages her tears had wrought. Then she went to check on Jane Westcott.

As she expected, she found Jane busy bringing herself to order and completely irritated with herself for allowing her emotions of the morning to get the better of her. She was in a flurry of dressing, preparing for a morning visit she had promised to make but had overlooked the day before. She accepted the news that Beth was going walking with Miss Rathsham with a "humph" of disapproval. When she had learned of Lord Rathsham's attitude after the race she had stigmatised him as gothic and fustian to a ridiculous degree and cut him from her list of acquaintances.

While Beth was thus occupied in assuring herself that Jane was not in need of her services, a footman brought up a message showing that Beth's concern was shared. Lord Farling had asked to be informed of when Mrs. Westcott might receive him.

"Oh, dear!" Jane plumped down on the edge of a couch, almost crushing a new, expensive, and very fashionable hat. "And I am expected at Mrs. Johnson's. What am I to do?"

"As you said, Jane, it's either feast or famine. I'll leave you to make your decision while I see to my guest."

By the time Beth returned to her sitting room, Miss Rathsham had eradicated the evidence of her tears with damp cloths and had rearranged her curls. The tea tray had been brought in and the footman was just leaving. Beth poured and sat listening to the plans of the ministering angel as the young lady decided on how she could best help Mr. Thorpe.

"Do try and see if you can get him to make his peace with his uncle," Beth said.

Miss Rathsham stiffened and gave Beth a look of reproach. "It's my place to let him know that I am still of a true heart, and will not falter in his adversity," she said. "If his uncle has treated him so shabbily, I am not persuaded that he should put himself in the position to allow it to happen again."

Beth bit back the stinging words that she most wanted to retort and tried to remember that this childish attitude indeed came from a child.

"But wouldn't you like to see Jonny more often? Ride with him in the park? See him at parties? If he makes peace with his uncle, your father could be brought around. Wouldn't that be much more comfortable than clandestine meetings?" Beth's spirits sank as the expressions fleeting in Miss Rathsham's large brown eyes weighed the advantages of an approved and comfortable relationship versus the romance of stolen moments. Clearly, the young lady was a reader of the most shabby novels.

When Beth judged the time had come for them to leave for Green Park, they put on their bonnets, took their reticules, gloves, and two of Beth's parasols and set out. Beth was careful to wait until what she considered to be the last moment, knowing that every minute they stood about in the park increased their chances of being recognised.

On the way there they experimented with the parasols, hoping that these, in combination with their wide brimmed hats, would keep their faces hidden from most casual onlookers.

It seemed to Beth that she was achieving the desired effect, but the younger lady, in dipping her sunshade and then raising it to peek under the ruffles, was drawing the very attention they wished to avoid. Miss Rathsham became more nervous as they approached the park and Beth's irritation fled. The girl was not being coquettish, she simply lacked entirely the ability to play her part in an affair of secrecy. As they approached the turn in the carriage path where Beth had instructed Jonny to meet them, she ruthlessly decided to use the girl's nervousness to make one more attempt to persuade her to draw young Thorpe back to his uncle.

"It is so overpowering to be doing something we know will be disapproved, isn't it?" she asked, giving her companion a sympathetic look.

Miss Rathsham's answering expression was pregnant with gratitude for the other's understanding. Beth hardened her heart and went on with her ploy.

"And what your parents are going to say about your being out alone I cannot think. Jonny must reconcile with his uncle. It isn't fair of him to put you in this position."

The remark about Lord and Lady Rathsham had struck home, as Beth was sure it would. She had deliberately left any mention of their disapproval out of the earlier conversations, salving her conscience by reminding herself that the benefits to all concerned could outweigh the harm. After all, the young lady was in for a severe dressing down for leaving her home unattended, Beth told herself. What could another hour or so matter?

On being reminded of her parents, Sally looked considerably frightened. She glanced over her shoulder and her steps, which had heretofore been unfaltering, were hesitant.

Beth was afraid she had gone too far with her prompting, and it seemed evident that she must either continue or have the girl turn and flee.

"Of course, if under your persuasion, Jonny does forgive

his uncle, you will be a heroine. Heroines always suffer for their efforts, of course, but it is so uplifting. Things always come about for them, you know.''

"Yes, they do, do they not? Captain Lewis of the dragoons said something similar last night.''

Beth wasn't sure whether the thought of being a heroine or the memory of the captain had brightened Miss Rathsham's spirits, but before long she was cheerful again.

Fortune smiled on them, for they had only entered the shade of a tree by the curve in the road when Trumbril came bowling around the turn and brought the carriage to a halt. The door opened and Jonny alighted, followed by Myra and Major Cable. Beth was irritated to see that the major had accompanied them, but after his attempts to keep Jonny from listening to her advice, she would have considered it strange had he not come to protect his interest. She was not at all clear about the viscount's financial state, but it took no great deal of intelligence to know that after introducing Jonny to the *ton*, Lord Alspeth would be forced, for the sake of his own good name, to pull his nephew out from the river tick. She was sure, after talking to Freddy, that when the time came to "fork over the dibs,'' the amount would be as large as Major Cable could make it.

"Oh, Jonny!'' Miss Rathsham tripped forward, her every fear forgotten as he strode up, taking both her hands in his.

"Dash it, Sally, you shouldn't have come,'' he said, gazing down into her face like a moonstruck calf. "Better that I should cut my throat than let any trouble fall on you.''

Major Cable had made a sketchy bow to both ladies and stood close to young Thorpe's side, observing the reunion blandly. "Ah, but young ladies know the romantic value of clandestine meetings, and what else adds so much to romance?''

The flickering of understanding in Miss Rathsham's eyes drove Beth into action. While she knew that she herself

134

would not be turned aside by Cable's oily remarks, she put no dependence on the young lady's ability to hold to common sense. Left to do his damage unimpeded, there was no doubt in her mind that the major would shortly have the girl on his side. Beth steeled herself to put a spoke in his wheel.

"Good morning, Major Cable." She smiled sweetly at him. "So very nice to see you again. I'm sorry we had no time to talk when last we met, and I did want to ask you about your army career. I have several relatives serving, you know, so I have an interest in our brave fighting men. Do come walk with me."

"Ah, my dear Lady Elizabeth." He returned her smile. "I am desolate that I cannot do so, but to leave our two young friends alone would be the epitome of indiscretion. We must think of Miss Rathsham's name."

Beth nodded in agreement. "I appreciate and approve your sentiments, of course, but you need have no fear. While you and I walk apart, Jonny and Sally may take another path, with my maid discreetly behind them. After such an effort to bring about this meeting, I do think it heartless that they may not have even a few moments together outside a crowd."

"Oh, let's do take a stroll," Miss Rathsham said imploringly to Jonny. "It will be quite unexceptional, I'm sure. Myra is the soul of sympathy and discretion, and I trust her explicitly."

Tempted by the upturned pleading face of his companion, Jonny ignored the objections of Major Cable and agreed. Beth stood watching the young couple as they strolled down a path, and after a hard look at her employer, Myra followed at a discreet distance. As unwilling as the maid might be, her look was as nothing to the anger that glinted in the eyes of Major Cable.

"Well, my *lady*," he said maliciously. "Shall we, too, follow at a discreet distance?"

She gazed innocently up at his blazing eyes and tight jaw and shook her head. "I think not. Their path leads among the shrubbery, and I do feel so confined in closed places. The lawn over there looks inviting." She indicated the area across the carriage path where the widely spaced trees created a dappling of shade on the large open field. They would be under the eye of the burly Trumbril, who had driven the carriage. "A lovely place for a stroll, don't you think." Nothing would entice her to be alone with this man in a sheltered spot.

"It is not at all to my liking," Major Cable replied. "I have seen too many such fields in battle, and would prefer to be within hailing distance of our friends."

"Oh, but they must find us most definitely *de trop*, and if you are indeed going to tell me about your war experiences, then would not the lawn be more suitable, since it brings back your memories?"

With one hand on his arm she started to cross the hard-packed dirt road. He moved reluctantly at her side. She could tell he was weighing the dangers of attending her and leaving the young lovers to themselves against Jonny's disapproval if he were to leave Beth alone and go after his protégé. Apparently he decided that to act in an ungentlemanly fashion might open Jonny's eyes, because he quickened his step and turned his attention to Beth.

Beth's throat ached with the desire to tell Major Cable exactly what she thought of a man who would lure a fledgling like young Thorpe away from his family, but she wanted to avoid a confrontation. It would be exceedingly uncomfortable to spend her time with him in a pitched battle. Even more, she was afraid her temper might betray her into saying something he could take back to Jonny and thereby destroy the only slender contact that might lead to a reconciliation with the young man's uncle. Unlike Freddy Rathsham, she put no faith in the chances of Jonny's fleeing back to the sanctuary of the family hearth and dropping his troubles in the lap of his father or Lord Alspeth. She had seen the pride in the boy's eyes. If he was driven too far, it was her opinion that he might go into a self-imposed exile until he righted his own circumstances—if he ever did.

As they crossed the road and strolled over the grass she smiled up at the major.

"Were you with Wellington on his Peninsula campaign? I believe I read somewhere that the meadows of Pozoblanco with their widely spaced trees and the lawns kept short by the grazing sheep were very beautiful. It must have been terrible to see such a peaceful place destroyed by a brutal battle. That was the action for which Wellington was given his first title, was it not?"

"You know your campaigns, I see," Major Cable replied. "You're right in every case, of course. But do consider that the duke's enemies thought themselves strategists enough to best him and were proved wrong. It is not wise to stand against superior numbers and experience."

Beth smiled and nodded as if she hadn't understood the threat underlying his words. She wanted to retort that a strategist knew his ground, which Major Cable certainly did not. Since her father had faithfully followed the war at the breakfast table every morning with the aid of the post and the local papers, Beth was reasonably familiar with the various battles. Major Cable's replies proved to her satisfaction that he had not been with the duke, or he would have known that Sir Arthur Wellesley had earned his title of Viscount Wellington for his bravery at Talavera and lived to tell of it by leaving his wounded men behind to be captured by the French. She had heard it said that his action was the expedient thing to do, but both the title and the battle that earned it had stuck in her mind because of the horror and shame she felt. In addition, she was unsure that the little mountain city of Pozoblanco—if indeed it was even large enough to be called a city—had ever been the scene of a battle. Certainly Wellington had never fought there. Beth had no doubt that the rank of major was no more real than the taradiddles she spouted for the amusement of the *ton*.

"Granted the duke was experienced," Beth replied innocently. "But I was under the impression that he often went against far greater numbers than could be counted in his own army?"

"In that case, my lady, his knowledge and wit aided him. When a man knows his field and lets nothing stand in his way, it's dangerous to try and stop him."

Beth was silent for a moment. He was not going to keep the gloves on, she decided, and there was no need for her to do so either.

"That could be, Major, but another, equally daunting trait is determination. It causes such a desire for victory that no stone is left unturned until the battle is won."

"Then the person of such determination had better take care, else when he or she turns up a stone, what is under it might cause her a great deal of trouble."

Beth gave him a straight look. "Yes, disgusting things do crawl out from under rocks, don't they?"

"There is always that danger when a person steps out of her element." The major's eyes glittered angrily. "Now I suggest that we recross the road and join our friends. If you think I'm going to let that little ninnyhammer cozen Thorpe into returning to his uncle, you don't have the wit I gave you credit for."

"Oh, she might." Beth stopped in her tracks as he reached for her arm and made a point of drawing it away from him. "And I have no plans to start a search that might prevent her from doing all she can."

"Then if you will excuse me." He bowed. "I will endeavour to do just that."

Beth laughed. "That wouldn't be very intelligent of you.

If you leave me unescorted you will offend Jonny's sense of gallantry. Of course, I should not have said that, I suppose. It would be to my advantage to show him a true picture of the type of company he's keeping."

Major Cable stood for a moment, looking indecisive. Then he turned to stroll along at Beth's side again. His sardonic leer made her want to shiver, but she forceably withheld it.

"For your sake as well as mine, you had better hope she fails. If I lose this pigeon, my lady, you may regret it."

"Sir, I am a farmer. I have never yet been bested by varmints that enter the hen house."

=11=

WHEN JONNY AND Miss Rathsham returned from their walk, neither Major Cable nor Beth could ask the question foremost in their minds. It was answered, however, when Jonny asked Beth if she would see the young lady home in her carriage and announced his intention of hailing a hack for himself and Major Cable. The only thing that gave Beth solace was the speculative look in Major Cable's eye. Jonny's attitude was subdued, and the major was obviously unsure his victory was complete. When he mentioned the romantic aspects of secret meetings, Jonny frowned him down.

The parting of the couple was painful for their friends to observe, and Beth counted on the tears Miss Rathsham shed to weigh on Jonny's mind. She was naturally disappointed that the girl had failed to bring the boy around, and had no illusions that there would be a second chance. Miss Rathsham had given Jonny her word that their meeting would remain a secret, but Beth seriously doubted the girl's ability to keep that word when faced with angry, questioning parents. Knowing Lord Rathsham's attitude, she was sure Sally would not have another opportunity to slip away unchaperoned.

When she left Miss Rathsham at her home, she returned to Berkeley Square to find both Jane and Lord Farling out. She retired to her room to plot her next course of action, but she was thwarted by Myra.

The maid, finding her employer at leisure, took the opportunity to draw Beth into the dressing room to discuss several repairs and needed additions to her wardrobe. What had begun as a decision over whether two flounces could be mended had developed into a general inspection of Beth's entire wardrobe. The room was littered with piles of mending, stacks of garments to be disposed of, and others that Beth wanted refurbished with trims more to her liking, when a footman announced that Lord Farling and Mrs. Westcott had returned and were having tea.

Beth found them in the drawing room. Her companion had fully overcome her upset of the morning, and Beth was pleased to see her in high spirits, colour in her cheeks and eyes sparkling.

"Jane, you look so well," Beth could not help but observe. "You appear to have had a most pleasant day, while I have been drudging over my depleted wardrobe."

"Oh, let's not talk of mundane things—not when I have had the most delightful day indeed, and not at all tiring." Jane glanced at Lord Farling and Beth saw the softening of her eyes. "Gubby says he's going to take us in hand. He says we have not caught the knack of surviving the season, and after one day in his company, I am convinced he is right. With him as our guide, I have no doubt that we can complete the season with less strain. You will not believe the tricks he has taught me in this one day."

Before Beth could elicit any further information, Hughes opened the doors to announce Lord Alspeth, making Jane's happiness complete. Beth's heart gave a skip as he entered the room, but her joy at seeing him was counterbalanced and then overweighed by the secret that she must keep from him.

"Steven!" Jane was on her feet, rushing forward to greet her nephew. "I'm so happy you're here. I have been so anxious to see you today."

"I can't think why, Aunt," the marquis said, smiling tenderly as he bent over her hand. "I have not been very good company lately."

"Oh, but you will be!" Jane said, leading him by the hand and walking up to where Beth sat. "Dearest, I did so want to leave it to you, but I'm so excited I can no longer stand it. Steven, guess what this clever girl has done—she's found Jonny!"

Beth had read the expression "and her bones turned to water," but it was the first time she experienced that particular weakness.

"Found Jonny?" she repeated, incredulous. She couldn't believe someone had learned her secret.

Jane caught Beth's hand in hers. "Oh, dearest, don't tease us. Lady Sayer had occasion to drive into Green Park this morning—she was giving her grandson a treat. He was on the way there with his nurse—well, never mind that. The important thing is that she saw you with Jonny. She's sure she wasn't mistaken—she knows you both. Do tell us, dearest Beth, will the boy come back? Must Steven go to him?" Jane gazed pleadingly up at her nephew. "You will, won't you, Steven?"

"Of course I will," the marquis replied. "I'm honour driven to do everything possible to make peace with the boy, for his sake as well as his father's—where is he, my lady?"

Beth dropped her eyes. "I'm sorry, but I can't tell you. I had to give my word I would not."

"Stuff!" ejaculated Lord Farling. He had been watching and listening with a complacent smile transforming his features, but at Beth's refusal to divulge the information he leaned forward, his face growing red. "Tell Alspeth where he'll find the boy and be done with the missishness."

"I can only repeat, Uncle, I gave my word!" Beth's frustration took refuge in anger. "The only way I could reach the boy was to promise not to divulge the location of his lodgings."

"Nonsense, damned silly business," Lord Farling returned, but at a quelling look from Jane he lapsed into an unintelligible muttering. Jane's countenance took on a hurt look, but as much pain as that brought Beth, it was the expression of the marquis that cut through her like a knife. Hope had overridden his first small doubts, but naked disbelief took over at Beth's refusal to answer the question. She watched as his eyes grew cold with anger. His voice was stiffly controlled.

"I think I understand. You haven't forgiven me for my misjudgement of the occurrence at the Farnham track. It seems I misjudged more than that. I was under the impression you spoke the truth when I offered my apology and you accepted it. I see I was wrong—but bear in mind, my lady, that when you leave Jonny in such straits as a green boy can get himself into in London, you are making him pay for my sins." With a curt nod that included both Jane and Lord Farling, the marquis strode out of the drawing room.

Beth sat, watching him go, feeling as if the entire world had dropped from beneath her feet. Never in her life had she felt as miserable as she did at that moment. Added to her pain was the look of suffering on Jane's face. With a sob she, too, fled the room. Beth sighed and buried her face in her hands, wishing she could find an outlet in a strong case of the vapours.

"Girl, I don't like you upsetting Jane!" Lord Farling rose and paced up and down the carpet. "I don't understand you. Why didn't you tell him? I thought you liked Alspeth."

"He is a very worthy gentleman," Beth replied, forcing her voice around the aching in her throat. "You don't know how much I want to tell him, but at the moment I am convinced it would do more harm than good. If he approached

Jonny at this time the boy would, I think, run away again, and none of us would know where he was. If I break my word to him he certainly wouldn't tell *me*, and he doesn't want his uncle to know. Jonny is heading for trouble, I think, but there is nothing any of us can do until he sees that the character he has taken up with is what Freddy Rathsham calls an ivory turner. I doubt he would listen to the marquis, even if that odious Major Cable gave him a chance.''

"You know the boy is in bad company? Beth, what has happened to your sense of right?''

"I gave my *word*—does that mean nothing to you?'' She gasped at the unfairness of her retort. "I'm sorry, Uncle, that was unkind and I didn't mean to cast aspersions on you. It is the measure of my concern that I seem to be losing my control.''

After a hard look at her he resumed pacing. Gradually the anger that consumed him ebbed and he came over to sit by Beth, taking her hand.

"It's a rare hobble you're in, dear. What's to be done? What do you see as the outcome?''

"I don't know, Uncle. Jonny adores his uncle, and I think his hurt can be measured in how he feels about their falling out. I think—no, it's not reasoning, it's only a hope—that he won't be long in coming to his senses.''

She told Lord Farling about her walk to Green Park with Miss Rathsham and her hopes that the romance would help to pull the young man back into the protection of his family. Lord Farling shook his head and voiced his disapproval of her abetting a scheme that would earn the censure of Lord Rathsham. He would have prosed on at length, but Beth cut him short, explaining that either she or Myra had been with the young lady at all times.

"Still don't like it—but I'm more concerned with the mischief the boy might get into,'' he grumbled. "Doubt that Alspeth will ever forgive you if anything happens to that boy that can't be mended. He's a man who values a good conscience and he's taking this hard. Something's got to be done.''

For the next two days Beth moved in a fog of indecision. In her every waking hour she changed her mind at least once as inside her head the battle between her word and what she thought to be right raged endlessly with her desire to please Jane and the marquis.

There seemed to be an agreement in Berkeley Square that the subject was not to be mentioned, but Jane, though she made no verbal pleas, could not refrain from casting the most pitiful glances in Beth's direction. Lord Farling, once he had considered Beth's position, had used no more arguments on her and made an effort to keep the company jolly. Since his nature was as straightforward as Beth's, his attempts at a gaiety he didn't feel only added to the general feeling of tension.

Beth's training carried her through a blur of social engagements. She searched through the travel books so that when the inevitable request for her outrageous tales were made, she was able to carry them off, creditably for the most part. Even the one time she became confused and told the same story twice was met with laughter and a great deal of quizzing.

It was not to be thought wonderful that the mood of the house on Berkeley Square soon drove Lord Farling to remember that he had promised a visit to a friend near Oxford, so on the third morning after the painful scene, he left London, promising to return within a fortnight.

That night something happened to lighten Beth's mood. She had seen no hope for reconciling Jonny with his uncle and easing the tensions that were making a havoc of all their lives. The rout they attended was a crush and the hot, moist evening was enough to completely overweigh Beth's lagging spirits without her initial interview with Mr. Rathsham.

The gentleman had approached her early in the evening, requesting that she save him a dance, but his face was a study of nonchalance that did nothing to cover his dark mood.

"Didn't l-like what happened with m'sister," he said under his breath. "N-Not your fault, of course, but the chit's got to get Jonny out of her m-mind. G-Going to the dogs. Can't l-let him take m'sister down with him, you understand. F-Family name and all that, you know."

"I'm sorry," Beth replied. "I had hoped that talking to her would make him realise how far he's putting himself from his family and friends. I saw that she was well chaperoned—" Her eyes flew up to his face. "They haven't met since, have they?"

"N-No danger of that. M'folks are watching her like a family of hawks with one chick. Her going didn't d-do the job, apparently. Giving up m'self. Not g-going to be s-seen in ramshackle company. C-Cause m'father to have apoplexy or something."

He made his leg and walked away, leaving Beth more depressed than ever. She was just turning back to Jane when she saw Lord Alspeth bowing over his aunt's hand. One look in Beth's direction and his smile froze. He bade her a good evening and took his leave of them, strolling away. When Mr. Rathsham came to claim his dance, he was blunt about mentioning the cooled relationship.

"P-Pretty shabby of Alspeth to blame you for Jonny's walkout," he said. "Thought the m-marquis was a great gun. Must've been mistaken."

"He doesn't blame me. He knows I've seen Jonny and thinks I'm keeping his whereabouts a secret out of spite."

They moved through the figures, parted, and came back together again in the dance, and for several minutes Mr. Rathsham remained silent. Then suddenly he smiled.

"That j-just might be the answer," he said brightly.

"What?" Beth, whose mind had been wandering toward

Lord Alspeth and his lovely partner, had entirely forgotten what she had said.

"That you are in tr-trouble because you kept your word to him. C-Can't believe Jonny's not enough of a gentleman to go to his uncle and explain that. T-Take the blame off you and g-get them together at the same time. Just the thing! I'll see him f-first thing tomorrow. Hadn't p-planned on seeing him again, you know. Won't put up with that ivory t-turner."

For the rest of the evening Beth danced on feet that carried no weight at all. When Jane noticed her changed mood she, too, lit with hope. Beth could not resist drawing her apart and confiding Freddy's plan to her.

"Will it work, do you think? Oh, it must!" Jane was in transports.

Beth grabbed her companion's hands in an excess of joy. "We are counting on it. Don't you see? If Jonny does as Freddy is sure he will, Lord Alspeth will be able to talk him around."

Jane rocked on the balls of her feet in her excitement. "I must tell Steven. He will be so pleased."

Beth tightened her grasp on her Jane's hands. "I'm not sure you should. Just think how disappointed he will be if our plan doesn't work. Do you want to raise his hopes for what might be nothing?"

Jane turned thoughtful. "You are right, of course. I must not. Oh, but I'm sure our troubles will soon be over and we can all be happy again."

As usual, Beth's dance program was filled, and when the music started her partner for the next dance came to claim her hand. When she left the dance floor she was accosted by Lady Castlereagh, who was circulating the latest fashionable *on dit,* so Beth was parted from Jane for the rest of the evening. She was leaving the floor with Mr. Coster after the last dance when she saw Jane and the marquis in deep conversation. As his eyes raised from his aunt's, he gave the room a searching glance, finding her and giving her the most friendly smile she had seen in weeks.

With the footmen and coachman within hearing as they were driven home, and their two maids waiting to rush them to bed, there was no time for further discussion that night. As soon as the door to the breakfast parlour closed on the servants the next morning, Beth questioned Jane.

"What did you tell the marquis? No hedging, Jane, it must have been quite a tale, since he looked as if he was willing to forgive me anything."

Jane smiled mischievously. "I am persuaded that your taradiddles are contagious, dearest."

"Jane! What did you say?"

Jane poured and sipped a cup of tea with an air of injured innocence. "Only what you told me—with a slight alteration. I said the idea was yours, and that you were counting on Jonny's sense of honour to bring him out of hiding. I did add that you thought having the boy come to Steven would be a much better arrangement than if he were run to ground as if he were a fox."

"I knew you were a sly one, Jane. I think you're the fox. We'll have to tell him the truth later of course—" She shook her head as her companion made to object. "No, Jane, I am convinced that to take the credit for the actions of others is the same as being a cutpurse, but for the moment we will not put any rub in the way of harmony."

Unfortunately, the rub was brought by Mr. Freddy Rathsham.

Less than an hour later, while the two ladies were at their correspondence in the small drawing room, the young gentleman's card was brought up by the scandalised Hughes, for the young man nearly treaded on his heels instead of waiting to be invited up. One look at Freddy's face told Beth that all their plans had been brought to nothing. Rising and hurrying to meet her guest, she dismissed Hughes, nearly shutting the door on his offended person as she turned on Mr. Rathsham.

"What is it, Freddy?"

"It's all up with J-Jonny," he gasped. "Something has h-happened. He w-wouldn't say what. H-He's leaving the country! N-No talking h-him out of it!"

"But what—why?" Jane came rushing forward, but so great was her agitation that she staggered and Beth was forced to catch her arm and help her to a chair.

"W-Wouldn't s-say," Mr. Rathsham reiterated. "M-Must be the devil of a c-coil, though."

"Steven!" Jane gasped out. "Beth, dearest, please, *please* go to Steven. He's the only one who can stop Jonny."

"Just the th-thing. N-Need to see him anyway," Freddy nodded emphatically. "Hack w-waiting at the door."

Without taking time to don either a shawl or a hat, Beth followed Freddy to the carriage, leaving a shocked Hughes at the door with an order to send Jane's maid to attend her employer.

In the vehicle, Beth made no attempt to get more information from Freddy. He was so overcome by his agitated stammer that she left him to compose himself. She hoped he could fully relate his tale to the marquis.

At Alspeth House a footman, more puffed up in the consequence of his employer than was the marquis himself, took one look at the two visitors and refused to disturb his master. Neither Freddy, with his hat askew and his neckcloth disarranged where he had been tugging at it in his discomfort, nor Beth, innocent of hat, shawl, reticule or gloves, presented a picture of the ideal callers.

Fortunately, the marquis must have been watching from an upper window, because he appeared on the second floor landing and ordered the footman to show his visitors the book room. As Lord Alspeth elected to join them immediately by the expedient of running down the stairs, taking the steps two and three at a time, the footman, cognizant of his employer's fall from dignity, stood staring with such a scandalised expression that the marquis himself led the way to the combination office and library. As he closed the door his eyes raked over his visitors, taking in at a glance their appearance, which plainly said that their call was urgent. To Beth, the set of his jaw was daunting, but Mr. Rathsham seemed to take heart.

"It's like this, sir. Lady B-Beth and I had an idea—"

"He knows all about that," Beth broke in. "Tell him what happened this morning."

"J-Jonny was up in the bows," Mr. Rathsham said. "My th-thought is that he has sported more blunt than was the thing—you know—"

"I doubt that," the marquis said. "Go on."

Mr. Rathsham shook his head. "Oh, quite p-possible! Took up with a Captain Sharp. Dr-Dropped a bundle. Q-Quite obvious."

"I take it you know very little about your friend Jonny," Lord Alspeth said crisply. "If he had dropped enough to put him in the river tick, all of London would have heard of it. He's no Golden Ball, but he's one of the warmest young men on the town. Added to that he's no gamester. He has no interest in gambling, so if an ivory turner has enticed him to drop a few guineas, he's earned his commission. If he's in trouble it has to be something else. What is it?"

Freddy seemed struck by the news. "That explains h-how he has the money to tr-travel then. Wondered about that. D-Didn't understand it, how he could be lurched and st-still have the d-dibs to cut and r-run, you know. M-Must be something pretty devilish then. Not the t-type to fly in the bows over n-nothing. Says he's making the ship th-that's leaving right away for America."

"What?" Alspeth was on his feet.

"Oh, and s-says you are to know where he's b-been staying. I'm to tell you and take Lady Beth off the f-fire. N-Not that it will do you much good. He was throwing things into his b-bags and sent his boy to find a h-hack."

The marquis crossed the room and jerked open the door, shouting for a footman. Mr. Rathsham divined his purpose. "If you're going to c-call for your carriage, I suggest we t-take my hack. I k-kept it waiting."

"I'll have my housekeeper escort you home," Lord Alspeth said, giving Beth the first fleeting attention of the morning.

"I'd like to wait," she replied. "Perhaps you will be bringing Jonny back here."

With another quick look he was gone, Freddy at his heels, and Beth was left sitting with her worries, wondering if they would be on time. A few minutes later a footman entered and suggested she would be more comfortable in the main salon, but Beth firmly refused. This room reminded her of her own office at Carthalin Hall. Hers would have shown at a disadvantage, since it was shabby by comparison, but it, too, was a man's room, furnished with a large and commodious desk, shelves for books and accounts, and great leather-covered chairs that were designed for comfort rather than fashion. Her office had been her father's and it always seemed that some of him lingered there. This room gave her the same feeling.

She shook away the idea, thinking it had to be the chairs, so like those she was accustomed to. Trying to distract herself, she perused the shelves that held many of the same books that comprised her own library. Only here, set apart from the others and ready at hand to the person occupying the desk, was the largest collection of works on horse breeding that had been her privilege to see.

She was grateful for the tea and cakes that the footman brought in shortly after Lord Alspeth and Freddy had left for

Jonny's rooms, but though she drank two cups of the perfectly brewed beverage, her throat rebelled at the food.

After what seemed an entire day, but by the clock was only forty minutes, there was a disturbance in the hall and Freddy dashed into the room.

"Th-Thought you'd still be h-here," he said, his stammer worse. "J-Jonny is g-gone! G-Got to look at that shipping l-list." Suiting action to words, he seized the paper and started turning the pages. In his agitation, he was flipping through so fast there was only a small chance he would find what he sought.

"Let me." Beth took the paper from him and turned to the sailing schedule immediately.

"The *Johanna* is due to sail from Portsmouth for New York the day after tomorrow. A Dutch ship. That's the only one listed."

"Then that narrows the field," Lord Alspeth said from the doorway. "I should be able to catch him on the road."

"I hope to heaven you can," Beth said, handing him the paper.

"Yes, I'm sure you do." The marquis's voice was harsh as he took the folded section and stuffed it in the pocket of his greatcoat. Without another word he turned and left the room while Beth stared at the vacant spot he had so recently occupied.

Was his unfriendly attitude because he was worried, or was he blaming her for withholding the knowledge of Jonny's whereabouts until the boy had fled? She had no doubt his coldness was caused by the latter. If he was unable to intercept Jonny before the youth left the country, she was sure the marquis would never forgive her.

$=\mathbf{12}=$

BACK AT BERKELEY Square, where she was escorted by a very worried Mr. Freddy Rathsham, Beth was faced with explaining to Jane Westcott that they had failed to intercept young Thorpe.

"Steven will catch him," Jane said positively. "Jonny had to travel in a post chaise with hired postillions. Steven most likely took his own cattle. He can catch him."

"Of course he can," Beth replied staunchly. Jane had spoken with an authority her trembling hands belied, but if she could keep her courage in hand, it was not for Beth to put forth her own fears.

Two days dragged by before they heard any news. It was impossible for them to send their regrets to the hostesses whose invitations they had accepted without raising gossip, so they reluctantly followed a rigourous schedule of social events. For both ladies it was torture to keep up a charming but inconsequential conversation when their minds and hearts were turned toward Portsmouth. On the third afternoon, while Jane was still dressing for their afternoon promenade, Beth had just stepped into the hall to speak with Hughes when there was an urgent knock on the door. The footman opened it, and Beth gasped as she recognised the tall, angular silhouette that stood out against the outside light.

"Jonny!" she cried, rushing to the entrance and pulling

the young man in. "We thought you had sailed for America!"

"Planned to," he replied in a tired voice. "May I speak with you? I'd rather not see Aunt Jane right now."

"Of course." Beth looked around and led the way to a small salon off the entrance that was seldom used. She closed the door and tried to take Thorpe's hand, but he moved away from her. Ignoring his reluctance to be close to her, she took a chair by the empty fireplace.

"I'm so glad you haven't left the country. If you would just make it up with your uncle everything would be fine again."

"Lord, I wish I had done it before," Jonny muttered. "That's why I'm here. I've got to see him." He moved restlessly. Watching him, Beth was shocked at his appearance. His actions had a nervous jerkiness and his eyes were sunken, darkened with shadows that made him look as if he had been ill.

"He's on his way to Portsmouth," Beth replied. "He'll be back as soon as he learns you're not sailing."

"Oh, my God—then it's all up with me!" He threw himself down on a chair with such force that the sturdy piece of furnishing creaked alarmingly.

Beth moved to the chair adjacent to his and put a consoling hand on his arm. "Jonny, if it's money I can help you—anything else I can do—"

"It's not money and don't *touch* me!" The last he uttered forcefully and jumped to his feet to resume his pacing. Then he seemed to realise he had injured her feelings, because he stopped his striding and turned an anguished face toward her.

"I'm not fit to touch. You don't know what I've done!"

"Whatever it is, Jonny, you have a loving family and good friends. We will stand by you."

"All the way to the gallows?" he demanded savagely. "I've killed a man! Will you uphold me in that?"

He stood in the center of the room, tensely upright. The burning intensity in his eyes was heightened by a shine of moisture. His fists were clenched. He reminded Beth of the young boys on her farms. The four-year difference in their ages seemed to stretch into centuries.

"No matter what anyone says, Jonny, I will never believe you could deliberately hurt anyone. It simply is not in your nature. Now tell me the truth. It was an accident, wasn't it?"

She had spoken with quiet assurance and for a long moment the young man stared at her, as if trying to find horror or disgust lurking behind her words. Her calm acceptance of his confession crumpled his belligerent stand. He came back to the chair and sat, leaning forward, his hands on his knees, staring unseeingly across the room.

"Mean to? I didn't even know the man. I don't remember it. Can you imagine that? I killed him and don't even *remember* it. Cable and I had been out at a gaming hell. I was drunk as a wheelbarrow—beg pardon, but no good trying to put a pretty face on it. Don't like gaming, never did, and I'd been scoffing blue ruin. He says I insisted on driving his carriage, and his friends agree. I knocked the old man down and killed him." He raised a tortured face to hers. "I killed him and I don't even remember it."

"I wouldn't believe a word Cable said," Beth argued. "And even if you did, it was an accident."

"No, it wasn't an accident," Jonny denied. "I didn't mean to hit him, of course, but it was a bit of larking that I didn't pull off. Earlier that evening—and I do remember this—we had been boasting about how we could graze the wheels off carriages, and this fellow Lawson and I were quizzing each other about lifting shopping baskets out of wenches' hands. Nothing but talk, of course."

155

"I'm certain of that," Beth assured him, encouraging him to go on with his story. "What happened then, or what does Major Cable say about it?"

"They say when I left that evening I insisted on driving his rig and tried to prove my boast. Not wenches with baskets, too late at night for that, but I did swerve to see how close to the old man I could come. Had done it to a couple of others before I came to him, Cable said."

"But you can't trust one word Cable says."

"Not a whit," came the bitter rejoinder. "I know that now. But in this case I don't have to. The next morning one of the people I had scared came and raised quite a dust. I'll have to give it to Cable, he got me out of the suds with that man, but if I have to stand a trial and that fellow comes forward, I'm done for. Done for one way or the other anyway."

"What do you mean?"

"It's Cable. He's a scab, and why I didn't see it before, I don't know. When I was ready to skip out—thought I could at least save the family a scandal, you know—not really trying to save myself, understand—rather go to prison than leave England—"

"Of course. I understand, but what happened?"

"He caught me before I could get away and then I really found out what he is. Damn cutpurse—begging your pardon again. He says he's got plans for me. I'm to shag back to Uncle Steven, go to all the parties and get the layout of the houses—find out when different owners are going to be out for the evening."

"Robbery!" Beth gasped.

"That's what he's got in mind, all right." Jonny nodded glumly. "And either I go along with him or he turns me over to the Bow Street Runners."

"You can't do it," Beth said decisively.

"I can't do it, and I can't not do it," the desperate boy muttered. "I'm in the devil of a hobble."

"I'm not sure it is a bad thing that the marquis is out of town," Beth mused. "They can't expect you to go back into society until he returns. That gives us time to think."

Jonny brightened a little, but his raised spirits were of short duration. "That's right, but it's only a delay. I need a solution, and that's why I was looking for Uncle Steven. I hate worse than anything to let him know about this, but he's a dashed downy one. If anyone can conjure a way out of this, he will do it."

"What if you were to go to the authorities? If they knew Major Cable was trying to blackmail you, they might think his evidence was lacking truth—it might make a difference."

Jonny shook his head. "It's just my word against his on the blackmailing, and do you think he's going to admit it? He's a smooth talker—be out of it in three minutes. I've got no proof on them, but they've got plenty on me. Lady Beth, what am I going to do?"

"Delay," Beth insisted. "Perhaps we can even get a message to Lord Alspeth and have him stay away from London for a few more days. If he understood your plight I know he would."

"But how could we do that—short of one of us going after him? Cable has allowed me a long leash, but I'm being watched, I know. If one of us shags off after Uncle Steven they're sure to know, and you can't send him a written message. Suppose it fell into someone else's hands? I might have another blackmailer to deal with."

Beth acknowledged the logic of this, but she was not willing to give up hope. As she had boasted to Major Cable, she wasn't one to allow varmints in her hen house without expending every effort to rid herself of them.

"We'll think of something," she said with more conviction than she felt. "What we need is a little time to mull this over. You go back to—where are you staying now?"

"I'm at Grillon's for the present."

"Then go back and try to rest. In your state your mind isn't working. Let's use the delay to explore the possibilities."

They returned to the hall and were just in time to meet Jane as she descended the stairs. The news that Jonny was soon to be reconciled with the marquis brought on more tears, this time happy ones. They were of short duration, because Beth chided her for making Jonny uncomfortable and insisted she had to gain control of herself before they took their afternoon stroll.

Jane's pleas for Jonny to accompany them met with a startled look and an adamant refusal. "Your social schedule is a little hectic for me," he announced, throwing an admonitory glance at Beth.

She immediately caught the meaning behind his words. If Major Cable had known of the relationship between Jane and Jonny, he would have demanded that the boy accompany the ladies, who would be even more likely to give him access to all the wealthier homes of the *ton*. Though no doubt Lord Alspeth received as many invitations as they, he could not be expected to attend as many engagements as a young lady in her first season.

Jonny announced his intention of leaving a note at his uncle's residence, something he had overlooked doing in his earlier efforts to run the marquis to ground, and abandoned the two ladies to their promenade.

Believing her major worries to be out of her life, Jane chattered incessantly on their walk. Her mind seemed entirely taken up with her relief and she gave Beth room for only an occasional monosyllable. Therefore, when they returned home with the express intention of dressing for dinner and a ball, Jane surprised Beth by following her into her dressing room and dismissing Myra. When she had firmly closed the door on the offended maid, Jane turned to Beth, every vestige of her complacent ignorance removed from her countenance.

"Have you been able to solve Jonny's problem, or would two minds do it better? He *is* my great-nephew, you know."

Despite her surprise, Beth gave a chuckle. "Jane, you are amazing. How did you know?"

"I didn't listen at the door, if that's what you had in mind," she replied. "But anyone could see that Jonny was very disturbed, and you have been preoccupied since he was here. You might as well tell me. I'm not usually a vapourous female, you know. It has been the helplessness of the situation that has overset me. Let me be of assistance, I beg of you. I'd only be imagining the worst if left to myself."

Beth thought it better to imagine the worst than to know it for a fact, but she kept her opinion to herself. She removed her hat and gloves, dropping the shawl on the bed, raking her fingers through her crushed curls. Jane stood watching her with an air of impatience that convinced Beth her chaperone was not going to be fobbed off with a simple tale.

"If you really want to help Jonny then I beg of you, ask me no questions at the moment. Instead, help me locate all the copies of the *Times* for the past week. I have an odious habit of scattering them, and what Hughes does with the parts I leave lying around, I have no idea."

"But—" Jane drew herself up like an angry hen, but then common sense seemed to take over and she pulled off her hat. "I will see Hughes, but then you will tell me," she muttered and sailed from the room.

Several times in the past weeks, Beth had read part of the paper as she drank her morning chocolate, and Myra, at the first opportunity, would whisk them into a bottom drawer of the chifferobe with the haste of someone removing dirty linen. Beth had removed them and scattered them on the bed, searching each page, when Jane returned with an armload. After watching quietly for a few minutes Jane ventured an inquiry.

"If you would tell me what you are searching for—"

Beth, finished with the scattered sheets she had taken from the chifferobe, took the stack of papers from Jane's arms and spread them in front of her.

"But that is just the problem, dearest, I can't. It's some vague memory of something I read—I must find it, but I'll only know it when I see it." She sorted the papers, opened one after the other, and scanned the sheets. A vague memory of a small notice nagged at her, but until she found it she wouldn't know what importance it had, or indeed, if it had any at all. Then she saw what she had been looking for and reread it avidly.

"Here it is. I thought I remembered it!"

"May I please know now?" Jane's voice was rising in pitch alarmingly. "I am persuaded that I will have the silly vapours again if you insist on keeping the secret from me."

With the paper in her hand, Beth put one arm around her chaperone's shoulders and led her to a pair of chairs near the window.

"Jane, dear, I have no wish to add to your troubles, so I had to have a glimmer of hope before I told you what Jonny told me, and what he believes to be true. You see, things are not so bad as he thinks." She told Jane the story that Jonny had brought her, hastily reassuring the little widow when her face paled.

" . . . and Jonny said it was on Farringdon Road. See here, the *Times* reports that a man was struck down on Farringdon Road that night. He suffered injuries to the head as well as a broken leg, but he is not dead!"

Jane read the short notice and looked up at Beth doubtfully. "But it could not be the same man. Surely Jonny would have made inquiries, or at least searched the paper for information. I cannot believe this accident has anything to do with my nephew.''

"Would Jonny have done so?'' Beth asked. ''Remember, he was at that time with that odious Major Cable, and the man is wily enough to keep a boy as upset as Jonny must have been from looking too closely into the affair. Then, too, look at where the notice was printed. They had a small space left over at the bottom of the list of cattle auctions. That is why I saw it, but who else would look for the report of an accident in such a place?''

Jane was still doubtful. ''Even if Jonny was too upset to be thinking clearly, Major Cable should have seen it.''

"He didn't impress me as the type who would read about cattle auctions,'' Beth said firmly. ''And even if he did, he would be the last to tell Jonny the truth. I have no doubt he arranged for the witnesses who convinced the poor boy of his guilt.''

Jane unfolded the paper to peruse the entire page. ''They most certainly did report the accident in a strange place,'' she said. ''Who would have seen it except farmers? Or someone expressly looking for a horse.''

"Just so.'' Beth patted her hand. ''How fortunate my major interest is still in my farms. I read the notices every day, and on Wednesday they were thin of material. I'm sure no lady read this receipt for currant jelly, either.''

Jane folded the paper and stood up. ''We must get word to Jonny right away.''

"I think not,'' Beth replied. ''First I think we should see the man ourselves. We must convince him not to bring charges against Jonny.''

"But how will we accomplish that?'' Jane looked worried. ''I cannot but expect to find him in a very bad humour over the matter, even if his injuries were not extensive.''

"The paper says he is in a small charity hospital. I've no

doubt he would like to see Jonny before the magistrates, but he might consider it more important to receive the wherewithal to see his recovery through in comfort. Sending Jonny to Newgate, if the case is that desperate, will not fill his purse." Beth cast a guilty look at Jane. "I will allow that I'd not attempt to buy the man's silence if it were anyone but Jonny, but I am convinced the boy has learned his lessson."

"I will go to see him right away," Jane decided and rose from her chair, but Beth caught her arm.

"Not you, Jane, dear. Myra and I will go early in the morning. While I may be known in society, I have not been in London long enough so that the rest of the population would know my face. You might be recognised and connected with both Jonny and the marquis. If we can manage the thing without using names, we are much better off, you see."

Jane shook her head. "I can agree with your logic, but I cannot allow it. I see here the hospital is virtually in the shadow of Old Bailey. That is no part of town for a young lady. Your uncle would never forgive me if I allowed you to go."

Beth folded her arms across her chest and tightened her lips. "Jane, this is something *I* must do. It was my fault the boy is in such trouble, and I must do all that is possible to help him. It is a matter of honour with me. I ask you to understand that."

The look of obstinacy faded from Jane's face too quickly to have been convincing. "You're right, my dear. Not that I think you were ever to blame, but if it will ease your mind to see this man yourself, I must allow you to do so." She picked up the paper and looked at the article again. "I suppose I must go and dress for dinner. I shudder at the thought of upsetting Mrs. Griggs by being late at table."

Beth watched Jane leave the room, uneasy at the sudden acquiescence exhibited by the lively little widow. When, only moments afterward, Myra came in and started laying out Beth's evening clothes, Beth bethought an errand and asked Myra to step down to the drying room to see to a particular pair of stockings.

Myra sniffed her distrust of the errand. "Ridding yourself of my presence, young lady? I wonder what it is you are up to now. If it's after that young rapscallion boy again, I'll not be fobbed off."

"I give you my word I am not," Beth answered calmly. "Not that you need telling, I'm sure, but from this evening on his place of residence is quite respectable and I could approach him any time without secrecy."

"I'm not one for listening to gossip, as you are well aware," Myra returned sharply. "Still Grillon's is no place for you to be going to visit a gentleman, young as he might be, and respectable a hotel as it is."

"And if you don't listen to gossip, how did you know he was at Grillon's?" Beth goaded the old servant.

"My *lady*, there is a vast difference between *listening* and *overhearing*!" With that cryptic remark, Myra flounced out of the room, closing the door with a force just short of a slam.

Beth gave a hiss of irritation. She had planned on catching it before it closed but she was a fraction of a second too late. She opened it cautiously, leaving just a crack so part of the hall was visible, and looked out. As she expected she saw nothing but the dim emptiness while Myra's angry footsteps echoed from the rear of the house, so she took the opportunity to possess herself of her dark blue domino and a pouch of coachwheels she kept by for emergencies.

Going back to her door again, she took up her vigil. Unless she was completely mistaken in her summation of her chaperone's character, Jane was going to slip out and visit the charity hospital alone, to prevent Beth from going on an errand she deemed unfitting.

Myra's footsteps had hardly faded away when Jane's maid

passed Beth's door. Knowing she was right in guessing her companion's intent, Beth donned her domino and slipped through the door just after Jane, similarly cloaked, had gone stealthily down the stairs.

Since most of the servants were either busy in the kitchen or about their own evening meal, Jane slipped through the servants' entrance unnoticed, with Beth close behind her. Jane was unaware she was followed until Beth stepped up beside her and spoke.

"This is ridiculous. I told you we should wait until tomorrow."

"Oh, drat!" Jane replied with no real feeling behind her words. "I meant to handle it myself. No one is going to bother me in a hospital, after all, and you should not come."

"If no one is going to bother you, then I should be safe," Beth said.

There was more difficulty than they had expected in finding a hack at that time of day, and the jarvey, upon hearing the direction, appeared thunderstruck.

"Lor'," he was heard to mutter as the hack moved off down the street. "Stap me if I hever 'eard tell the like! Gentrymorts a'going to such places."

It was well after sunset when they had left the house, and nearly dark when they had located the hack. Beth felt some hesitation about going into doubtful parts of town in the evening, and her every misgiving was reinforced as they left the fashionable section. Jane, too, seemed daunted by the class of people passing along the dirty streets, and she cast several apprehensive looks at Beth. In order to bolster her chaperone's courage, Beth sat straighter, raising her chin to show her confidence, wondering if she might jack her head off her shoulders if their ride was much longer.

Beth was thinking, too, about the consequences of their slipping out of Berkeley Square. Since both ladies had retired to their rooms and then summarily disappeared, it would not be surprising if quite a dust was being raised. She could rely on the servants she had brought from Carthalin Hall to remain quiet, but how much London servants gossiped had been made readily apparent by the number of times Myra had brought Beth tales about their neighbours. Myra's ability to overhear things she refused to listen to was a constant source of amusement to Beth, but it also showed her how much reliance she could put in keeping this venture from becoming an on-dit in society. There was no help for it, she would be in another scrape.

The jarvey pulled up in front of a decrepit-looking building, though it was apparent from its size and the proportions of the entrance that it had once hoped for a proud future.

"I'll not be liking it, that I won't," he grumbled as he opened the door and let down the steps of his vehicle, which had once been a private coach. "Leaving gentrymorts in a place like this ain't right to my way of thinking."

"Then don't leave us," Beth replied as he handed her down. "We'll not be very long inside, and there will be another of these if you wait and take us back to Berkeley Square." She gave him one of the coachwheels from the pouch inside her reticule. The gratuity was outrageous, she knew, but cheap enough when she considered the alternative—having to search for a hack in that particular neighbourhood after dark.

They climbed the steps to the first floor entrance and walked into a dimly lit foyer. A battered table, on which several record books and an ink stand reposed, and, behind it, a rickety chair, were the only furnishings. As she moved toward them, Beth saw through an open doorway to her left, a long, narrow room with six or eight beds along one wall, all of which seemed to be occupied. She had turned in that direction when a woman dressed in grey appeared in the doorway and curtly asked their business.

She was a tall, gaunt woman with an air of authority and the lines on her face indicated she was not given to smiling. She eyed the two women, obviously fashionable despite their dark garments and hidden faces, and disapproved of what she saw.

"We are here to see the gentleman who was struck down on Farringdon Road," Jane said promptly.

"I see," the woman replied coldly. "Relatives, if I may ask?" Her sneer made a reply unnecessary.

"Is it possible to see him?" Beth asked. "We read about his accident in the paper, and would like to ease his circumstances."

The matron sniffed, making her disbelief obvious. "There's many here that's more deserving of help than that one. I'll take you to him, but what you have to say, you'll say in my hearing. I'll have no shady goings on while I'm on duty."

With another disapproving look at their concealing capes she led the way across the entrance hall, up a staircase, and into a smaller ward on the third floor. All but two beds were empty, and the man nearest the door was snoring heavily.

The matron led them to the bed at the far end of the room, where a man lay staring out the window. There was a bandage around his head and his right leg was splinted, its bulk clear under the frayed blanket.

"Some ladies to see you, Simms," the matron said as she stopped at the end of the bed and made room for Beth and Jane to approach.

The emaciated man turned a suspicious eye on Beth and Jane and nodded casually. "Mighty pleased to have the company."

"We were indeed sorry to hear about your accident," Jane commiserated softly. She would have said more, but the sinister smile that lit Simms's face stopped her.

"Oho, accident, is it?" He leered at Jane. "I was wondering just how I came to be receiving gentrymorts. Now I see how it is."

"Mind your manners, Simms," the matron snapped. "Seeing as how these ladies are offering to help you, a civil tongue might be to your advantage."

"Weel now, that it might, and it might be to my advantage to ask of you to summon the authorities. Hi there, Jackson! Wake up down there and bear witness!" This last he shouted, bring the sleeping man at the other end of the room awake with a start. Then he lowered his voice and looked hard at Jane.

"So it was some high-up swell that ran me down. Knew it all along, and here you are, my lady, a'wanting to buy your loved one out of trouble. Mighty fine of you, my lady, mighty fine feelings on your part."

Beth glanced back down the room to see the other patient on his elbow, turned and listening intently. The matron, too, was considering what Simms had said, and it was clear by her expression that she was of the same opinion as the stricken man.

"What you say is true, of course," Jane said. "That is why I am here, but I come persuaded, no matter how it must have looked, that you were struck by accident. The person who was driving that carriage would never harm anyone deliberately. You can summon the authorities, of course, and you will have your revenge, but even that will not make him regret the incident any more than he does now. On the other hand, if you can find forgiveness and admit it was an accident, I will be more than glad to make your convalescence easier."

"How easy?" Simms licked his lips, avarice glittering in his eyes.

"A hundred pounds?" Jane suggested.

"Arr, what do you take me for, a bleeding flat?" Simms nearly shouted. "The likes of you can do better than that, I warrant."

Beth stepped forward, but Jane, who stood between her and the patient, reached out her hand, holding her back.

"You make a mistake, Mr. Simms. We are not wealthy. We are simple working folk like you—"

"Working folk!" the matron scoffed. "Not this cut-purse!"

"It's you that'll be keeping your chaffer closed!" Simms glared at the matron and then turned his anger on Jane. "You'll do better than that, me fine lady, or it's to the authorities I'll go. Not that I'll be knowing who *you* be, but the bloke as drove that rig is a cove I've been seeing around, and always with quality. Oncet I'm on my feet agin, I don't misdoubt I can find him. There's no missing that short, square frame of his, and I'll be remembering he's around those gaming hells where the young gentry hangs out—"

"Short—square frame?" Beth interrupted.

"Aye, didn't think I could have got that good a look at him, did you, miss gentrymort?"

"Then it *wasn't*—" Jane clapped her hand over her mouth to keep from blurting out Jonny's name. She sagged against the bed behind her and gave a deep sigh. Beth stepped closer and put one hand on Jane's trembling shoulder, thinking she might faint, but Jane, divining her purpose, assured her she was quite all right.

Then Beth turned to the matron, who was staring at the three as if they had all taken leave of their senses.

"Matron, I do think if Mr. Simms wishes to speak to the authorities, he should by all means be allowed to do so." She delved into her reticule and pulled out the purse of coach-wheels. Counting out ten, she dropped them on the bed in reach of Simms's nearer hand. Five she handed to Jane with instructions to give them to Jackson, who had been listening as closely. One she kept for the driver of the hack, but the rest she gave to the matron.

"For your work here, and if you are questioned by the authorities, I beg of you to tell the truth as you have heard it here tonight." She bade the startled Mr. Simms a good evening and turned toward the door, where the second patient was somewhat dazedly thanking Jane for the unexpected largesse.

As they descended the stairs they could hear Simms, who had found his voice, cursing over losing what he claimed could have been thousands of pounds. Jackson, who was disposed to think of the visitors kindly, was laughing and warning him that his lofty ideas would earn him a knife in the back for his greed.

The matron's initial disapproval had dissolved with the pouch of coins in her hand, and as she followed the ladies down the stairs she murmured about extra blankets and another ward maid between her curt hoarse thanks. To Beth, whose resources were admirable, the almost two hundred pounds was a bargain for the gratitude that would certainly stand Jonny in good stead if Simms decided to change his mind about who was driving the carriage.

As they reached the foyer the matron hurriedly placed the purse in the drawer of the battered table and walked with Beth and Jane to the street, where their hack awaited them.

"God bless you both," she said again as she hurried forward, opening the door on the vehicle before the driver could reach the ground. "Go safe home, and know that you'll be remembered in my prayers."

"I'm so relieved." Jane clapped her hands as they clattered off down the street. They sat back, relaxing, Jane with her blissful sighs, Beth trying to think up some tale that would satisfy her servants. She was not much worried on their account, knowing that what she and her friend had learned that evening would more than make up to her for any idle gossip that might circulate.

Still it would be wise to prevent any talk that she could, and to visit Grillon's hotel and give the news to Jonny would not only ease his mind, but would give them an innocuous excuse for leaving the house. What reason they would have for slipping out and taking a hired hack, she could not think, but it would be unexceptionable for Jane to visit a relative and for Beth to accompany her.

She was leaning forward to tap on the side of the hack and give the driver directions to go to Grillon's when the vehicle slowed and turned, going between two large doors into a dark, cavernous building.

"Driver!" she shouted. "What is this place? Why are we here?"

The hack came to a halt and a light from a lantern pierced the darkness. The door was jerked open, and the light fell on both Jane and Beth inside the carriage and on Major Cable, who stood just outside. He smiled evilly up at Beth.

=13=

BETH STARED AT the short man in the dandified clothing. The danger of the position in which she found herself had not yet entered her mind, and she was only concerned with his presumption in opening the carriage door.

"How dare you?" she demanded. "I'd advise you to get away from this vehicle in short order, or you'll be in more trouble than you are already."

His smile widened. "I once told you, my lady, that it was dangerous to oppose a man on his own ground. It's a pity you refused to listen." The smile disappeared. "Will you get out, or shall I have my men remove you?"

Beth stepped slowly down from the hack. She cast a dark look in the direction of the driver and stopped short in surprise. The hat and coat were the same, but the face was not that of the jarvey who had driven them from Berkeley Square.

"Did you injure my driver?" she demanded, sure the man would not have given up his clothing as well as his vehicle without a fight.

Major Cable shrugged. "If they did you might take the blame yourself. Shameful of you to buy a man's loyalty when it might mean his death—but then you think money can do anything, don't you, my lady?"

Beth saw no purpose in answering his question, since she was not the one who would blackmail and rob. She glanced at the big doors, wondering if there was a chance she and Jane could escape, but the entrance was even then being closed by two of Major Cable's minions. Jane had stepped down behind Beth, and she looked the major over haughtily.

"Why are you bothering us? Who are you?"

"You'll get your answers soon enough," Cable snarled. "I want to know how Thorpe found out where they took the man he ran down. I hadn't found him yet myself."

"Who—" Jane started to say, but Beth interrupted to keep her companion from blurting out what they had learned.

"He didn't. We found him—but he had already succumbed to his injuries," Beth lied, hoping to prevent Cable from taking the man's life to prevent him from telling the truth.

Major Cable's eyes narrowed. "That's coming on a little too thick, girl. Thorpe tells you what happened, loses the man I had following him, and right away you go to the charity hospital? If I hadn't sent Jake to Berkeley Square to pick up Thorpe's trail in case he came back to your house we would have been properly gulled. Don't tell me he didn't tip you on where that bloke was being treated."

"Well, he didn't, but he didn't need to," Beth rejoined. "If either of you had read the *Times* you would have known." She pulled the folded paper from her reticule and handed it to the major to convince him of Jonny's ignorance. What good it would do, she didn't know, but at the moment she was buying time. Behind her, one of Cable's men grew impatient.

"Arr, enough of this talk. Let's get rid of them and be on our way."

"Not so fast." Cable looked thoughtful. "If she's telling the truth and Thorpe doesn't know what they've been up to, then we'd be fools to throw over a promising operation. Take them in the back and tie them up. If he meets us and we can bring off the job, we'll take them out on Finchley Common later. No point in letting Thorpe think we had anything to do with what happens to them."

Cable turned and started for the back of the warehouse, and as the lantern he carried had only one side unshuttered, Beth was unable to see who caught her arm and roughly pulled her along after him. Behind her she heard Jane complain that she was being pushed too fast over the uneven floor, but the pace continued until they reached the end of the building, where the single lantern dimly illuminated a small, dirty office, which held only a high table and a tall stool. It seemed to Beth that the building must be abandoned.

Rough hands pulled the sash from her dress and tied it over her mouth as a gag. Then she was pushed to the floor and bound hand and foot. Twice Cable adjured his men to hurry.

"You think the whelp will really be there?" one of the others asked.

"If he isn't we'll run him to ground and get rid of him at the same time we take care of them," Cable replied. "At least we won't have to worry about the lady of the house being in."

The others seemed to find something funny in his statement, but Beth was too busy testing the ropes to pay much attention. When she realised her captors were leaving, she twisted around, searching for anything that might help her free herself, but the lantern was taken away too quickly and she despairingly watched the dim glimmer as it receded down the length of the long building.

Nor could Jane help her. Cable, with a joke about Jane's age, which Beth was sure was less than his own, had ordered the widow tied upon the tall stool, her feet bound to the rungs.

The footsteps sounded farther and farther away, and with

the echo of a door closing, Beth knew they were alone in the darkness. No one was being left to guard them, but as she tugged at the ropes, she felt as they must that there was no need to spare a man.

Beth twisted, shifting her position, trying to ease the strain on the ropes. Across the room she heard sounds of creaking wood that at first she could not identify, but a muffled grunt informed her that Jane was attempting the same task.

They had been at work for some time when Beth paused. The sound of tiny pattering footsteps alerted her to the unwelcome presence of rats. She shuddered violently, hoping they would not enter the small office. Then she was alerted to another sound—the jingling of a harness.

Cable and his men had left the hack in the warehouse, the old horse still harnessed to it. Like humans, horses have no love of rodents. It was, she knew, a foolish rat that would try to cross the floor of an occupied stall.

Gagged though she was, she murmured soothing sounds as loud as she was able. The horse, like all its kind, would be uneasy in a strange dark place, missing its owner and longing for its stall. Her efforts were rewarded by a questioning whicker and after several more tries she heard the slow steps as the animal moved hesitantly in their direction, pulling the hack, which had a squeaking wheel. Beth hoped to draw the horse close to the door to protect them from the rats.

"Oh, goodness, that's better," Jane said breathlessly "I've worked my gag loose," she unnecessarily informed Beth. "Dearest, are you all right?"

"Uh-huh," Beth replied and went back to her urging of the horse, who was drawing nearer. Along with trying to free her hands and feet, Beth gave more thought to the gag, rubbing the knot against the floor. Presently she too was able, by working her chin and pushing against the knot, to free her mouth.

"Come on, boy," she urged the horse as soon as she was able.

"Why are you calling the horse?" Jane asked with some dismay. "If he can enter, won't he likely step on you? I think you should leave him where he is."

"Don't worry, Jane," Beth replied. "He won't be able to get in the door." She didn't want to add to Jane's distress by bringing her attention to the rats. "He's free, you see. I'm comforted just because he's there."

"I daresay I should have become more familiar with horses, if one can bring about an ease of mind, but I confess, if he cannot cut these ropes, which is asking too much, I find him a bit *de trop*."

For more time than Beth liked to think of, they worked in quiet, each trying to loosen her bonds. Beth felt the ropes give as she pressed her arms together behind her back, and with fingers that were growing scratched and sore from the rough hemp, she managed at length to slip one hand free. Wriggling and twisting, working one arm out, she eased the strain on the knot that held her left wrist and felt the rope uncoil.

"I have a foot free," Jane announced at almost the same time.

Beth freed her feet by taking off her boots, and hurried across the floor in her stockinged feet to help Jane. In a short time the widow's bonds were off, and they felt their way to the door of the abandoned office.

"Back! Back," Beth urged. She pushed against the horse pressed against the door, as close to the two women as his harness and shafts would allow.

"Get into the carriage," Beth said to Jane. "I'll lead him to the door." She realised she didn't have her boots, but decided not to risk going back for them. If Major Cable and his men were out on a robbery, they would soon be back.

"You lead the horse," Jane proposed. "I'll move ahead and find the doors. It would be so helpful if we could find that lantern. How long do you think we've been in here?"

"Too long," Beth replied. "Try for the doors. There is a bar across them. I noticed that before they took us into the office."

Beth's unhopeful words on the time proved to be prophetic. As they crossed the warehouse, she leading the horse and hack, Jane walking some distance ahead, a small door at the side opened and a lantern flashed. Into the warehouse came Cable and three of his men. Beth stopped, hoping they would not at first see her and Jane, and they might still have a chance for escape, but Jane, out in the open and wearing a light green dress, was fully illuminated in the dimness.

"Get those women!" Cable shouted.

With a growl, a big, red-bearded man ran after Jane who, with the light of the lantern to aid her, made a dash for the double doors and struggled to raise the bar from its brackets. Ignoring the rough floor that bruised her unshod feet, Beth urged the horse on, trying to block Jane's pursuer with the bulk of the animal and the hack, but she was a fraction of a second too late. While Jane tugged at the heavy timber the man grasped her arm and jerked her back from the door.

"Leaving our company, ladies?" Major Cable came up, his pistol aimed at Beth.

"Just stepping out for some air," Beth replied coldly. "We find something lacking in your hospitality, Cable." In the light of the lantern she was quite pleased to see the tightening of his jaw at her omission of his rank.

"Get the ropes," Cable snarled. "Tie them up again—and gag them properly this time. I'll have no more of your sass, woman."

Just as the third man started for the office, the door

behind Cable burst open and, in the dim light, Beth saw four men enter, pistols drawn.

"Hold there!" cried an authoritative voice. "Stand as you are in the name of the law!"

Jane squealed and succeeded in breaking away from her captor, after landing a hard blow to his shins with her boot. He jumped back and the little widow scampered back into the darkness of the warehouse.

Beth, on the other side of the carriage, could hear some scuffling and two shots. Major Cable swore and took shelter behind the wheel of the hack. He made a grab for Beth's arm, but jumping quickly away, she climbed into the carriage and slammed the door. She had no clear idea of what she could do to help her rescuers, but at least she would not be used as a shield.

Through the window of the carriage Beth saw the dim outlines of men scurrying to take cover behind several broken boxes. Then one figure, more clearly defined than the rest, left his cover and raced for the protection of an overturned barrel. Loose debris on the floor tripped him, and he fell sprawling in full sight of Major Cable and his men. Not until he gave an outraged oath did Beth recognise Jonny, as well as the tall, elegant marquis as he went to his nephew's aid.

As Beth peered through the window, a movement drew her attention and she saw Cable, his pistol in his hand, fixing his aim in their direction. Without thinking of the consequences, Beth threw open the door and jumped out, seizing Cable's arm. With a curse he pushed her aside, knocking her to the floor.

Did the lanterns go out? she wondered as darkness and unconsciousness overtook her.

Beth's head seemed to be spinning somewhere above her shoulders, and she wondered idly if, when it had occasion to resettle itself, it would be facing the right direction. The odour of musty cushions was the next thing to penetrate her awareness, and she slowly realised she was in the hack again, lying back against the squabs. Opening her eyes, she saw a very concerned Jane just opening a vinaigrette. Beth pushed the box away and tried to remember what had happened.

"Are you all right, dearest? No, don't try to sit up. Everything is quite over with, and we are going home."

"What happened?" Ignoring Jane's attempts to keep her prone, Beth sat up, peering out of the carriage. She was in time to see several unknown men leading Major Cable's three henchmen away. They were carrying the major between them.

"Oh, it was the grandest thing!" said Jonny, who stepped closer to the door of the hack. "We've got them all now. Off to Old Bailey with them—all but Cable. Hospital for him."

"I am delighted that it was grand," Beth said wearily, leaning back again on the cushions. "Since we had to go through all this, I would have been very put out to have it only middling."

"But it had to be magnificent." Lord Alspeth looked in the opposite window, smiling first at Beth and then through the carriage at Jonny. "The Thorpes don't do anything half-way, do they, puppy?"

As Beth turned to see the marquis, she noted that his coat had been removed, and a man in a dark grey suit was occupied in affixing a bandage to his upper arm.

"You've been hurt!" Beth cried and attempted to climb out of the hack, but Jane's grasp on her arm prevented her.

"I must speak to you about that," the marquis said, grinning. "I do most certainly appreciate your desire to save Jonny from a bullet, but did you have to pull the man's arm around so that he shot me?" He laughed at her thunderstruck expression. "It's only the veriest scratch, my dear. I won't heed it at all, once the blood stops trickling down my sleeve, and the good Mr. Belcher is at present taking care of that." As if to prove the point, when the task was finished, Lord Alspeth pulled on his coat unaided.

The lamps of the hack, now lit, added to the illumination in the warehouse, and in their glow Beth saw that even though he had sustained an injury, years seemed to have fallen from the face of the marquis. On the other side of the carriage, Jonny, watching through the other door, was looking inordinately pleased with himself as he attempted to tuck in one end of his neck cloth, which had been trailing down the front of his coat.

His dishevelment brought Beth's attention to herself and she gazed down at the filthy rumpled dress that had been torn and stained beyond repair in her struggles on the floor of the abandoned office. Raising her feet, she saw the torn stockings and remembered her pledge to her uncle that she would dress fashionably in London. Eyes brimming over with laughter, she turned her gaze on Jane, who was only in slightly better conditon.

"Dear Jane, do you think we can set another fashion style?"

The sudden release of weeks of worry, and of the tensions and terrors of the night, broke from Jane in a series of giggles that Beth immediately joined. Their impromptu mirth was brought to a halt by the clattering on the street of a carriage driven in haste and careening to a stop. Out of the fashionable vehicle bounded a very upset Lord Farling. He charged into the warehouse, his walking stick held before him like a weapon.

"What is the meaning of this?" He bore down on Lord Alspeth.

"Oh, Uncle, don't start being fustian." Beth dissolved into the giggles again. For some reason she was unable to fathom, his immaculate attire as he stood in the shabby warehouse struck her as extraordinarily humourous. "We are only enlivening the on-dits of the *ton*."

Lord Farling ignored his niece and turned his anger from the marquis to Jane. "Dashed fine business when a man can't go out of town without coming back to find his house in an uproar, and all the servants in hysterics, crying that we have been robbed and someone is making off with his niece and her companion. Told you before, Jane, you've not got the wit to be in town on your own. Don't know why I ever let you chaperone my niece."

Jonny had moved around to the other side of the hack, and he stepped into the light. "Now that's coming it a bit too strong, sir!"

"It most certainly is, Uncle," Beth put in. "Poor Jane has been through quite enough tonight."

"Dashed well would say she has! Think she's been through enough with one week of you, m'girl."

Beth was ready to retort, but Jane's nails biting into her arm silenced her as the plump little widow wrinkled her brow and her bottom lip quivered.

"Oh, you are so right, Gubby. I tried, I really did, but I think I needed your help all the time." She held out a suddenly trembling hand for Lord Farling to assist her out of the hack.

He nodded, his anger softening into concern as he pushed back a wayward curl that had fallen across her forehead.

"Obvious to me all the time. Can't trust a little chit like you to be able to handle everything." He took her arm and started for his carriage. As if it were an afterthought, he stopped and looked back at the marquis. "Alspeth, I trust you can get my niece home without any more to-do?"

"I'll try, sir," Lord Alspeth said with surprising meekness.

As they headed for the carriage Jane's voice floated back across the warehouse. "Now I feel really safe, Gubby."

"There, there, m'dear."

"Well, I say!" Jonny ejaculated as the carriage pulled off. He turned to Beth and the marquis with lively astonishment. "That's the most surprising turn-up of the evening."

"Only because you're such a puppy," Lord Alspeth replied, grinning as he watched the carriage out of sight. "The story is that Aunt Jane and Lord Farling were attached in their salad days, but my grandfather wouldn't allow the match. The earl was a younger son. Why do you think Aunt Jane was so set on being Lady Beth's companion? What better way to rekindle an old romance?"

Mr. Belcher, who had been singularly quiet though all the explanations, stepped forward, removing his hat and scratching his head.

"Uh—interesting and gratifying it might be, but I was needing to ask the lady a few questions. Need something for my report, you see." Beth recognised his voice as the one who had called out in the beginning of the gun fight, and decided he was a Bow Street Runner.

"Then I suggest we all retire to the Haughton-Marshall house, where the departed lady is now being taken. Lady Beth will be more comfortable in her own home."

"Aye, that she would, and it would be my pleasure to drive her there, since she's paid me handsomely for it in advance," said another voice. The speaker stepped into the light, and for the first time Beth realised it was the jarvey who had driven Jane and her from Berkeley Square. She was aware that he had been the fourth man to enter the warehouse, remembering the gleam of a white cloth around his head that she now saw to be a bandage, which did little to conceal the large bump on his head.

"Oh, you poor man." Beth looked at the injury with concern. "Are you sure you feel up to it?"

He waved away the idea. "Pay no attention to that, miss. Deserved it, I did, for letting them get the jump on me.

Came to, I did, just as the carriage rumbled off, and followed on foot. When I seen there was six of them I made to go for Bow Street, not that I have much truck with the law, you understand.'' This last he said with a cautious look in the direction of Mr. Belcher. ''Bit unsteady on my feet, I was, and I fell against a building. That did me in for some time, and when I came to I was not about to go where they might think as I'd held off coming, so I went to Berkeley Square, thinking as how you would have menfolk to come to your aid.''

''You'd have saved some time and his lordship a sore arm if you'd done as you knew you should,'' Mr. Belcher grumbled.

''He arrived in time, and that's the main thing,'' Beth said firmly. ''Now if you are sure you want to drive me home, I would be honoured.''

The marquis rode with Beth in the hack and let a delighted Jonny drive the team of chestnuts, accompanied by Mr. Belcher.

During the trip from the warehouse Beth put her head back on the worn squabs, suddenly shy of Lord Alspeth, and too tired to overcome her feelings. He, too, seemed fatigued and as they passed under the street lights she was aware of the mud on his clothing. Had he driven back from Portsmouth, only to be involved in a robbery and rescue? she wondered.

In Berkeley Square her servants were still in a turmoil and, completely ignoring the commands of Hughes, most of them were milling around in the entrance hall, awaiting her return. After her experiences of the evening, Beth was not in the mood to allow them any more than a glimpse of her before she summarily sent most of them to bed and ordered tea for herself and Jane as well as something stronger for the gentlemen.

In the main drawing room they found Jane and Lord

Farling, sitting side by side on a confidante. The joyous expression evidenced by Jane and an unusual awkwardness on the part of Beth's uncle told the full story.

Beth and Lord Alspeth were followed into the room by Jonny and Mr. Belcher, who took the center of the floor, looking around from one to the other in some confusion.

"Your pardon, but a report must be made, so I'll have to be asking some questions to clear up a few points."

"Well, I for one could not keep my mind on my answers unless I understood what brought all of you together to the warehouse," Beth said.

"I had just arrived here from Portsmouth when Jonny and Mr. Belcher came down the front steps, and together we encountered the jarvey," the marquis answered.

"How did Mr. Belcher and you get together?" Beth asked Jonny.

"Oh, Cable and I were robbing you," the young man said with superb nonchalance.

"You were what?" Lord Alspeth sat up straighter, and Jane, with a moan, buried her face in the lapels of Lord Farling's coat.

"Now, you'd better explain yourself, young master," Mr. Belcher said hastily. "It's upsetting your people something fierce, you're doing." He looked uncomfortably at Jane and Lord Alspeth. "A great help he was. Set it up so we could catch those fellows good and proper. About the accident on Farringdon Road, well, I think the magistrates will be easy with him, seeing what he's done to aid us."

"But he wasn't driving that carriage!" Beth announced. "Still, I don't see how being involved in a robbery could help with that."

"I wasn't driving? Are you sure?" Jonny looked stunned for a moment. "That's dashed good news! And about the robbery—it wasn't exactly that, you see. After our talk I knew what I needed was proof. So I did a bit of thinking and took my fences backward, you might say, trying to lose the fellow who was following me. Then I did a bit of the high toby on Mr. Belcher, here.''

"You held up a Bow Street Runner?'' The marquis nearly choked on his question.

"Ain't something I like admitting, you understand. It's likely to make me the laughingstock.'' Mr. Belcher frowned at Jonny, who put on an expression of angelic innocence. "Caught me in an alley—made me think he had a pistol in his coat pocket.''

Jonny took up the story. "You've got to understand, Uncle Steven—I couldn't be a part of Cable's plans. I'd rather stand my trial. Lady Beth gave me the idea by saying if I could prove blackmail then maybe the magistrates would think the testimony against me was trumped up. Anyway, I spilled the entire story to Mr. Belcher, and told him I could prove it, because Cable was going to break into the Haughton-Marshall house that evening. While his back was turned I skipped off and went to arrange it with Cable. It was easy enough, since I knew he was aware I had been there earlier in the day.''

"You mean he *hadn't* planned it?'' Belcher's face was getting dangerously red.

"Well, he was going somewhere sometime.'' Jonny looked astonished that the policeman would take offence. "I just made sure he would go where you were watching.''

"Dashed good idea,'' Lord Farling announced with authority, but he threw Jonny a dark look. "Don't care much for your choice of houses, however.''

"Oh, I thought Aunt Jane and Lady Beth were going to some party or another,'' Jonny explained. "Lucky that since they didn't, Cable took them off our hands. Wouldn't want them where they might get hurt, you know.''

"Thank you for your consideration,'' Beth said weakly.

"Knew you'd be a good sport about it." Thorpe gave her an approving smile, then sighed happily. "Glad it's all over, though."

"I think I have had enough answers for tonight," Jane spoke up. "Gubby, would you be so good as to see me upstairs to my maid? I don't feel very steady right now. My nerves are strong, but any more disclosures and I promise to have hysterics."

"Of course, my dear." Lord Farling led her out of the room while the others watched in silence. When the door had closed again, Beth turned to Jonny.

"I'm so happy it's all over. Now if we can just convince Lord Rathsham that you are a hero, you can see Sally again and all will be well."

"See Sally?" Young Thorpe started as if someone had shot at him. "Why on earth would I want to do that? She fancies herself in love with some dragoon now, I think. Silly chit! She thought it was romantic that I was in hiding and we had to meet secretly. Shabby way of doing things—I didn't care for that, I can tell you. Besides, I've got something else in mind. Quite a lark we've had, saving everybody being upset and all." He turned an engaging smile on Mr. Belcher. "I've been thinking. Everyone needs something to do to keep them from being bored, and you and I make a pretty good pair. How about it, if I join you—unofficially?"

"Wouldn't be at all the thing." Mr. Belcher shook his head emphatically.

"But think of what we could do," Jonny persevered. "I could be the gull that the Captain Sharps try to talk into things, and you would be on hand to—"

"Now see here, young master, that is not the business of someone like you. You could have gotten yourself killed—" The Bow Street Runner was backing toward the door, stalked by an enthusiastic Jonny, who interrupted his objections.

"That doesn't signify. A fellow has to learn to take his fences. Think what a team we would make."

Over the young man's shoulder, Mr. Belcher threw a desperate look at Lord Alspeth and Beth, who were laughing at his discomfort.

"I'll be back to ask my questions tomorrow, my lady," said the runner. "I think you've had more than enough excitement for tonight." He reached behind him for the door handle.

"But you don't understand at all," Jonny was saying as he, too, disappeared into the hall. "Think what larks we would have, and we'd become famous . . ." His excited voice faded away along with the hurried footsteps on the stairs.

Lord Alspeth rose and crossed the room to close the door before coming back to Beth.

"Tomorrow I'll have to rescue Bow Street before my nephew demoralises the entire law enforcement system, but tonight I have other matters to discuss." He caught Beth's wrists and pulled her to her feet. With one hand resting on each of her shoulders he gazed into her eyes. "I think the misery of this entire episode was that because of my own foolishness and my black moods over Jonny I nearly lost you. Still, I don't think I knew my own feelings until tonight when I learned you were in danger."

"But it was all my fault," Beth insisted. "My mad antics were at the root of all Jonny's problems. I thought you would never forgive me."

The marquis shook his head. "The foolish things we think—but that's all behind us now. Back in the days before our troubles began, I had a talk with Aunt Jane, and she told me your requirements." He removed one hand from her shoulder and reached into a pocket from which he pulled a stiff white piece of paper. His voice became very businesslike. "At Alspeth Manor, my principal seat, I have fifty-six layers, thirty-five pullets and seventeen setting hens. At Crompton

Farms I have thirty-seven layers—" His eyes, as he looked over the top of the paper, twinkled. "Is it necessary that I read the entire list, or will the fact that I know the productivity of my hen houses convince you of my eligibility as a husband? I'd advise you to accept me."

"Oh, you gudgeon!" Beth laughed and jerked the list from his hand and threw her arms around his neck. Then she realised what he had said when he was naming his properties. Her eyes widened in amazement.

"Crompton Farms!" she gasped. "The best breeding stable in the country is yours?"

"I plead guilty," he replied, smiling. "I like to spend most of my time there, but don't be downhearted. There is room for more chickens. We might even make some of them into hunters. Is that experimental enough for you?"

"That is indeed experimental enough," Beth answered, yielding to his kiss.